Yielding Ice
About to Melt

Richard Penna was born in Cornwall in the UK. He has lived and travelled in Greece and now lives in the south of France. In 1999 he published the prose-poem entitled *One Man.*

YIELDING ICE
ABOUT TO MELT

Richard Penna

Dufour Editions

First published in the United States of America, 2003
by Dufour Editions Inc., Chester Springs, Pennsylvania 19425

Cover Art: '*The Sea of Time*' by William Blake
Arlington Court (The National Trust), NTPL/John Hammond

Page 8 quote: From TAO TE CHING by Lao Tsu,
translated by Gia-Fu Feng & Jane English,
Copyright ©1972 by Gia-Fu Feng and Jane English. Used by
permission of Alfred A. Knopf, a division of Random House, Inc.

ISBN 0-8023-1339-6

Library of Congress Cataloging-in-Publication Data

Penna, Richard
    Yielding ice about to melt / Richard Penna
        p. cm.
    ISBN 0-8023-1339-6
    1. Physicians--Fiction. 2. Women--Fiction. I. Title

PR6116.E56Y54 2003
823'.92--dc21   2002192837

Printed and bound in the United States of America

Chapters

The Characters

Thomas . . . . employed in the house

Frieda

& . . . . . elderly twin sisters, owners of the house

Maria

Nina . . . . a cook

Genia . . . . an abandoned child

Elena . . . . a young governess for Genia

Christina . . . . a blind sculptor

Bella . . . . an ex-missionary

Rebecca . . a sick woman confined to her room

"Watchful, like men crossing a winter stream.
Alert, like men aware of danger.
Courteous, like visiting guests.
Yielding, like ice about to melt."

— Tao Te Ching

One

I sat as usual in the deep gloom at the back of the café, where I was uninterrupted and could, if I wished, observe the other people unnoticed; and being well away from the window I was less aware of the rain, falling heavily now, and less conscious of the sound of the great river gliding by a short distance in front of the building.

In the semi-darkness I groped inside my overcoat for my wallet and opened it flat on the table before me; though made of canvas this wallet was so old and so deep in grime that it had the appearance and feel of leather. It had been issued to me on the other side shortly after I had qualified as a doctor and was on the point of being drafted into the army; it still contained the papers, the certificates and passes, so typical of that time. But I had no great wish to be reminded of those days.

I indulged in a ritual, the high point of my week perhaps. My second glass of wine was on the table before me. Looking about me to make sure that I was alone and unobserved, I slid the tattered photograph of Christina from the wallet.

Ten or more years ago she stood in the shallows at the edge of the river, probably in the area known as the cove just to the north of the house. She wore a plain brown bathing costume and she held something like seaweed up towards the sun so that she could inspect it more closely. She could see, she was not yet blind.

As I sipped the wine and stared at the photograph the sense of loss grew within me and my eyes began to fill with tears. My love was so intense, my memories of her so tragic.

I thought of her painting that she had had to give up, and of the clay sculptures that she made now; thought too of the way in which she had turned in her chair only yesterday and fixed her eyes on me and had asked me a question, something about her work; and how I had been unable to reply, unable to speak because I so yearned to kiss her eyes and kneel in front of her and lay my head in her lap and feel her stroke my hair. I wanted above all that she would ask me to take her away from the house and the women; and my fantasy created the certainty that during our escape she would in the purest sense love me; she would discover that she was in love with me. Those thin white limbs would be above me and the long fair hair fall over me; and with her blind blue eyes and with her nakedness she would learn to know me.

Gradually I calmed myself, wiped my eyes. When the waiter came in my direction I called out for coffee;

when he brought it to me I saw that he had cut his finger and he dripped blood all the way to the table. Carefully I put away the photograph and replaced the wallet in the inside pocket of my overcoat. To distract myself I began to watch the other people drinking in the café. They were mostly men who had once been fishermen. When the fish had no longer been able to survive in the river they had pulled their boats up on the strand at the edge of the small town and despite the pointlessness of the work, they had spent much time caring for the craft, keeping them in good condition and painting them in traditional colors. But one winter a few years ago a fire was started on the windward side of the boats and in a single night they were all destroyed. Since then they have passed their days in the café, in aimless talk, aimless walks, and in sleep; there was nothing else to do.

I was interrupted in my thoughts by the old man who owned the café; he appeared from the shadows somewhere behind me and leant close to me and gently placed his hand on my shoulder.

"Thomas, if you don't go soon, with this rain the road will be impassable." I nodded my understanding and thanks for his warning, though I knew it and had heard it a hundred times during the winters of these past years. And there followed the usual thoughts; I could stay in the town, tell them that by the time I had loaded the truck with all the provisions, the road was already flooded. One day I would not return.

What finally forced me out into the lashing rain, checking the tarpaulin that covered the supplies, finding out if the battered old truck would in any case start at all, was simply the thought of Christina, alone and so vulnerable in that isolated house at the mercy of the weather and the women. Perhaps I thought too of the child, Genia, of her innocence, and of Nina, her laughter and warmth; and perhaps too of Frieda, her silence and strength. But Elena, Bella, Rebecca and Maria were strangers to me and I had no desire to see them ever again.

It was essential to complete the first part of the drive as quickly as possible in order to take advantage of the fairly good surface of the tarmac road; the last few miles were dirt track, full of potholes and liable to subside or wash away in very heavy rain. I made good progress until the last few miles when I was forced to slow to a crawl. The old truck's headlights were poor and it was loaded down with the extra weight of provisions in case I was unable to make the journey on the following week; sometimes in the depths of winter the road became totally impassable. After an hour wallowing from pothole to pothole I caught sight of the lights of the house.

At this point along the track, a mere two or three miles from the house, there was a violent wind blowing from the south–across the river, across the road and into the forest, lashing the trees into furious movement. There seemed no logical reason for the force of the wind. The river here turned slightly and at its greatest width was a little over a mile; the house was built in the apex of this bend and at this time of the year a large triangular sand bar built up directly before it. Around the house there were a few small native trees but on the side opposite to the river, always referred to as the back of the house, there was the large, unnatural cherry orchard, the trees unpruned and grown massive; for a few days in the spring the blossom was beautiful, but the trees bore no fruit.

Beyond the orchard, running the length of the river was the endless strip of level scrubland, difficult to walk in, and containing at regular intervals the mushroom circles indicating where the large old trees had been cut down many years before. And beyond that, the forest itself, for hundreds of miles, deeper than anyone knew, the forest that once grew right to the edge of the river, now cleared back; the forest, declared at some time in the past to be a conservation zone, and then, because people were discouraged from going near it, becoming completely forgotten and abandoned.

Many years ago, disillusioned with my world but filled nevertheless with a youthful energy, I abandoned the practice of medicine without having really started; in the spring of that year I managed to get a passage on one of the fishing boats that had been blown across the river during a storm. I returned with them to this side, to the small town with its sparse population and its inhospitable climate. I was pleased to be away from people and to have escaped from the overcrowded city and I found this country both beautiful and frightening.

Now, years later, I had no strong feelings about it either one way or another.

In the beginning I had a room in the town. I had no plans. I would spend days simply watching the great river surge quietly on towards the sea. In those days the river was blue and gray, the colors of the sky, and in the shallows there were all kinds of shellfish and snails and bright green flowering weed. Later, after I had moved into the house, we swam in the spring and summer in the small cove that was just upstream. If you let yourself float, a benign current carried you in an endless circle within the cove, out to the main flow of the river and then casting you almost casually back along the edge of the sand.

But the river had been polluted now for a long time, a filthy brown soup, sometimes giving off a sickening smell, sometimes the wind gathering yellow froth from its surface and flinging it at the windows of the house and onwards through the cherry orchard and still further into the forest itself.

After about a year or so in the town I met Frieda who asked me at once if I could drive and whether or not I wanted a job. A few months later I moved into the house that was occupied then only by Frieda and Maria; though the two elderly women were twin sisters, they were very different in every way. Frieda, it seemed, had acquired the house and had been joined at a later stage by Maria.

The arrangement suited me well since it meant that I could live cheaply in a fine house in a dramatic and isolated place while preparing myself for the future. I needed time, and peace and quiet. I thought of myself as an explorer, self-sufficient and strong; I thought that I knew myself well enough, both the good and the bad. I believed that the starkness of the landscape, the chill of the house, the pleasing sense of detachment from the women, could all be used to my advantage. I thought that I would soon overcome my anxiety, that it was merely a matter of time; then I would pack my bag and set off along the edge of the forest, searching for the right moment to plunge into its depths, to put the river and the house and the people behind me forever; if necessary to fight with the beasts of the forest, to win battles; to emerge finally into a new world, a new light...

But the years passed and little by little the situation in the house became more complex. At first I took on more duties. These were easy enough, tasks such as cutting wood and keeping the boiler going, repairing the jetty, looking after the boats and so on. But at the same time the old women began to add new people to their household; clearly the house was large enough to accommodate them all.

First, because both Frieda and Maria disliked cooking, they brought to the house a young woman from the town whose name was Nina. Then from somewhere else, an abandoned child, Genia, and within a few months Elena from across the river, a governess and teacher to look after her.

Next came Christina, the mysterious artist looking for a place where she could work quietly; the beautiful Christina who so loved to swim in the river and who persisted despite our warnings. She came back from the cove one day and her eyes were red and burning and as we sat with her during that night she became slowly blind. She could not cry. She wandered slowly in her studio studying her paintings for the last time. But I felt then only a great pity for her; I was not yet a victim of those moments of overwhelming desire.

After Christina came Bella, a missionary whom Frieda had found languishing in the clinic in the town.

A strange being, Bella recounted stories of the tribes who lived deep in the forest; according to her she had narrowly escaped from one such group which had unaccountably reverted to savage behavior and threatened her life.

She was followed within a year by Rebecca, also from the clinic, who was obviously seriously ill. Frieda required us not to question her but to leave her in peace until she had recovered and I had no clear idea of where she came from nor what was the matter with her. Rebecca did not recover but spent most of her life asleep in her bed in what we came to call the sick room.

Had it not been for Christina I would have left the house long before. Though I knew that she had no strong feelings for me, nevertheless I was convinced that she needed my presence; or rather that for some unknown reason, I should not desert her. And this sense of duty applied to a lesser extent to those others whom she loved; Genia, who helped her so often; Nina, who looked after so many of her practical needs; and Frieda, strong and remote, who so often read to Christina during the long winter darkness.

I had no deep relationship with these women, not even with Christina; and apart from my weekly ritual in the café, I felt that I had no healthy or positive feelings about them. But though I believe that I left them alone, did not interfere with their lives, they on the contrary, would not let me get on peacefully with mine.

They seemed to accept my presence casually, in a manner that was itself intrusive. They did not, for example, lock doors; they had no modesty. Even Frieda, whose dignity and age demanded some purity in her relationship to me, seemed not to care what I saw or heard or felt.

I lived in constant doubt about their feelings, their possible reactions in each new situation. This carelessness, this ambivalence towards me, created an atmosphere in the house that was always volatile, always dangerous. There was no vein of conduct on which I felt I could rely.

Yet despite all this, I was assailed by a desire to appear wonderful and strange and mysterious to each of them; to please them all. And in each day I felt only a sense of inadequacy. In varying degrees I disliked them; but at the same time I was endlessly curious about them, desperate perhaps to find a way to be more powerful than them; wanting perhaps to find a way to undermine them. But it was I who was gradually weakened, I who was only half alive.

The rain and wind increased their fury, striking the truck with such strong gusts that it was almost stopped in its tracks. I could see lights flickering in various rooms of the house, and in particular I could make out the lights in the balcony room reflected through the enormous windows onto the wet stone of the balcony itself. In this room I knew that Genia, or perhaps Genia and Elena together, would be laying the large table for the evening meal. I began to think of the smell of cooking in the kitchen and to imagine Nina's busy, strong, concentrated body moving between the kitchen table and the stove; her large mouth moving quickly, the words coming out quickly as she expressed irritation that I was so late with the provisions. But I knew that she would realize that I had had a hard and difficult drive and that I would need most of all to get warm and clean and dry; with a mocking tone she would push me out of the kitchen in the direction of my room; my dark room looking out onto the columns that supported the balcony, always shaded by the balcony, protected from rain and sun and moon, having only a narrow slit of a view of the rocks at the river's edge and beyond that out over the great level expanse of the river itself towards the indistinct horizon, the meeting of the dark water and dark sky.

I was still a short distance from the house, still wrestling with the cold metal of the steering wheel as it spun and shuddered in my hands; still imagining throwing off my wet clothes and climbing into a hot shower when suddenly every light in the house was extinguished. Utter blackness as if the house had never existed, with only the truck's feeble headlights illuminating the track a few feet ahead of me. In such weather this power failure was almost a certainty, but nevertheless I shouted out an oath, hardly audible above the roar of the engine, and I went on shouting it out until I reached the house itself.

Nina, an old shawl thrown over her head, appeared at once carrying a hurricane lamp. One by one I unloaded the boxes from the truck and carried them into the kitchen while she moved in front of me or behind me with the lamp to guide my way. But the gaiety and welcome that I had imagined and hoped for were not there; she was no happier than I about the power failure, though to call it a 'failure' was a misnomer; the power supply, always unreliable, had simply been switched off somewhere. On these occasions, since we had neither candles nor paraffin to waste, it was the custom for all of us to assemble in the balcony room and there, by the light of two small lamps, to wait patiently, and often in silence, for the power to be restored.

When I had showered and changed my clothes I followed Nina up the cold stone staircase and entered the balcony room on the floor above.

As I went into the room I was vaguely aware that many of the women were wearing long dresses and I wondered for a moment if I had forgotten some occasion, some anniversary, some reason why this was a special day; but I could think of nothing and so presumed that it was merely coincidence that they had all dressed themselves so elaborately. There was a vacant upright chair near to the fire and I sat on this and began to warm my hands. I put another log on the fire, wanting it to blaze more brightly. The room was vast and with only the two small lamps on the long table in the center, it took some time for my eyes to adjust to the dim light.

Some of them were sitting at the table, others on the chairs and sofas arranged around the edge of the room. They sat in silence, hardly moving.

Frieda, wearing a black dress, sat imperiously at the end of the table, her chair turned slightly towards the fire. Her hands rested lightly on her thighs, the fingers turned inwards, not an impatient posture as one might have assumed, but one of self-containment and stoicism. It was impossible to fathom this old woman. I gathered

more from Maria than from Frieda herself about what
little history there was. She had come across the river
with a man who had been killed or who had disappeared; her twin, Maria, had come across to be with her,
either to help her search for the missing man or else to
console and comfort her. At that time they were middle-
aged. When they heard of this desolate, isolated mansion
(which Maria insisted was built on the site of a castle),
they first rented it and then bought it, apparently having
no intention or desire to cross back over the river.

In the poor light I studied Frieda's profile, the severe
line of the mouth, the short cropped hair, the general
impression of intelligence and power. And though I knew
how she passed her days and what gave her pleasure—her
books, music, debate and inquiry—nevertheless she
remained a great mystery to me. At no time did I feel
that I made contact with her; there were no genuine feelings of sympathy. She did not seem to relax. And though
she was kind, even gentle sometimes, and considerate,
and admirable, despite these qualities the years of our
acquaintance had left us total strangers to each other.

Maria was sitting in an armchair and trying desperately, almost silently, to catch the attention of Genia,
probably to get her to come and sit by her; but Genia
was resisting, averting her eyes and turning away from
her. All the tension and strength that existed in Frieda's
body was completely lacking in Maria's. She was a large
and ample old woman and in another place, in other circumstances, would have been tight corseted; as it was her
body moved freely within the silken stuff of her dress.

She seemed much older than her sister and her long
black hair was held up in a loose bun and ribbon

arrangement, some half-hearted coiffure by one of the others. Her huge nipples were erect for some reason, and I could not understand how arms that were so fat... but Maria could not be described in this way, it was unwise. Certainly she was not as intelligent as Frieda, but she was no less powerful than her. Indeed it was the obvious pleasure she took in her own power that made her so different to the others; this combined with the fact that on the other hand she was completely oblivious of how repulsive she could appear; her voice, her manner, her possessiveness, her body, her odor, her familiarity could engender such a deep disgust; a disgust too profound to be voiced.

She believed that she, and she alone, was responsible for Christina's well-being. She would never let her alone, spoiling her for the others and for me; denying Christina, because of her blindness, the right to exist independently. And Maria believed too that it was her duty to be the guardian and guide to Genia in spite of the fact that Genia had no need of her... Yet Maria was a clever woman and it was impossible to speak to her; as long as there was reason within the truth, she would be deaf to all that was said to her.

Sitting on the sofa not far from Maria, Elena had one arm laid gently around the shoulder of Genia. This pose, mistress and pupil, governess and child, was very familiar and Elena was perfectly suited to the role; her serene, pale and beautiful face, her fair hair neatly plaited, the small head on the slender, elegant neck, the straight back, the sharp hands—the entire flesh and bone of the young body made human and soft and delicate by the fine clothes which added texture and form.

There was a book open in her lap though it was impossible to read in the feeble light.

Her eyes moved swiftly from Maria, whom she hated, to Christina, whom she loved, and on to me. No doubt she was dedicated, even devoted to Genia and that she looked after her with great care and discipline; but it seemed to me, particularly in her relationship with Christina, that there was an evil in this young woman, and I was forever wary of her. I disliked the fact that she rarely laughed, or even smiled, except with Christina; I resented their complicity, the obvious pleasure that Elena took in the secret nature of their relationship. It was impossible to trust, or even to like someone whose behavior was so consistently elusive and exclusive, and I was forced to conclude that she wilfully stirred up hatreds and rivalries and that her essential character was therefore malignant.

Genia, sitting by her, had beautiful brown eyes. She was perhaps eleven years old. But what could any man, especially a man who was not the father, say or think or feel about this child who was becoming a woman. I could only observe this strange metamorphosis at a distance, sometimes allowing the brown eyes to haunt my dreams. Only on the previous day she had come out onto the jetty where I was working and because the boards were still loose in places she caught hold of my hand and did not release it until we were safely back on the shore; I thought then what a tragedy it was that she could not swim in the river, her young body twisting and turning, cavorting and diving. And what a pity it was that I did not have a photograph of her. And what an honor it was that she allowed me to be so innocent and normal and free in her presence.

Almost at my feet on the rug before the fire, Bella knelt in complete stillness in an attitude of prayer. But whether she prayed or not, or whether she ever prayed, I could not have really said. With her own hands and with only a small amount of help she had refurbished the small chapel on the floor above. There she spent many of her days and her nights alone, in quiet chanting, praying and meditation.

As her procurer, inevitably I knew her secret, her drug addiction; but there were other strange aspects to her behavior that no one else seemed to want to question. To what god did she pray? And what was her religion? And what had happened to her before she had escaped from the violent tribe, and what had happened to the other missionaries?

At that moment she suddenly sat back on her heels as if she had awoken from a trance and began to look about the room; she found my face and smiled at me, obviously relieved that I had returned from the town with her package. Her black eyes were incredibly intense, though at that time the whites were dull and bloodshot. Her skin was dark brown, almost black, and there were deep scars on her face that must surely have been either some form of decoration or else the marks of an initiation; perhaps it was too wild, too violent a face to be thought beautiful.

From what I could understand, it was during her long conversations with Frieda that she had been persuaded to renounce her missionary work; and was that also the point in time when she grew her hair and began to wear long, heavy gold earrings? She was a private being, and she spoke little. Sometimes she stole things from our rooms or from the bathrooms or kitchen. But no one was keen to challenge her; and Nina warned me that only a madman would approach her.

Nina sat opposite to me and the firelight moving on her face made her appear very young; her skin seemed soft, as if covered with the down of childhood. She was clearly tired after her day's labors and her hands were curled upwards in her lap as if they ached and she tried to rest them. Her body was sturdy, with the appearance of great strength in her forearms and shoulders. And though this strength was of vital importance and the whole house depended on her in many ways, nevertheless her other less obvious skills were rarely remarked upon: her uncanny ability to find herbs and wild flowers in the scrubland; her ability to predict the weather, or the time of day, or the coming of illness, or to know the whereabouts of anyone at any time.

I suppose that it was true, as they said, that before coming to the house she had been a prostitute in the town. I saw her much more, or more regularly than the others, in part simply because my room was near to the kitchen, but this did not mean that I knew her better than the others. Strangely, despite our intimacy, she did not seem to me to have substance as a being; I did not know what gave her deep happiness, nor even deep sadness; I had not seen her cry, nor had I ever seen her face completely free of the slight and seductive smile. To me she was peculiarly transparent...

I got up then quickly and crossed the room as if I intended to look from the window. In front of Christina

I stopped and asked her quietly if she was cold. She turned towards me, smiled and shook her head. My reason for approaching her had been that she was so far from the guiding warmth and sound of the fire that in the silence of the room she had lost her sense of direction. She had turned slightly in her chair and her blind eyes faced the blank wall.

Rebecca, of course, was in her bed. If indeed this had been a special evening, no doubt she would have been dressed and I would have been asked to help her downstairs to the balcony room. As it was, I could be certain that she lay quite still, neither fully asleep nor awake, in her room at the top of the house.

I suggested that it seemed unlikely that the lights would be switched on during the evening, and that therefore there was no point in waiting any longer; it was decided to abandon the formal meal at the table, and instead we stayed where we were sitting and simply ate some fruit and drank some wine.

One by one they drifted away, disappearing into the darkness of the house. When I pulled back the curtains I could see the rain lashing against the window and hear the wind racing across the river and whining through the stone balustrade of the balcony. I put the guard on the fire and extinguished the lamps.

Two

I went to my room in the basement and lay on the bed. When at last an hour or so later I was convinced that the house was quiet I went out to the truck and from the cab floor rescued my flowers. I had been able to bargain for four flowers from the travellers in the town, not very fine specimens, somewhat battered and unfresh, but nevertheless real flowers. In the kitchen I trimmed each one and carefully wrapped the stems individually. There was a yellow rose and one black, one white and one purple tulip.

Going back upstairs I passed the balcony room and went on up to the floor above. Outside the studio where Christina also slept, I stopped and listened; I did not want to surprise her. But the heavy, nailed door was ajar and I could hear voices, low voices talking excitedly and quickly and with laughter. I recognized Christina's voice, and that also of Elena. I moved silently into the open doorway from where I could see that the room was illuminated by a single candle; I caught a glimpse of Elena's naked back as she sat on the edge of Christina's bed, and I saw her begin to lean forward towards the pillow on the bed.

I was bitterly disappointed and angry that I had been thwarted in my desire to give the rose to Christina; I had imagined her touching and smelling it. I had already experienced the pleasure that it would have given her.

Lighting a candle, I made my way to the floor above. I took the white tulip into the room at the end of the corridor, the so called sick-room. The room was in the tower of the original building and its heavy old door and stone cold walls seemed an unsuitable place for Rebecca to spend her life; but apparently she had early on insisted that she wanted to be in this remote corner of the house.

As I entered I was met by the strong odor of an unaired room which mingled with the sharp smell of some sort of medicine. I stopped quite still for a moment in the darkness, almost unable to breathe. Rebecca was lying on her side, facing me. I knelt down by the bed. She was in her usual state, neither fully awake nor properly asleep. I put the candle down on the bedside table and the light fell harshly on her wild red hair and on her face; a ghostly face, ashen, with dark pockets in the cheeks and around the eyes; and her lips, which hardly moved as she recognized me and breathed my name, were also colorless and lined with gray. She reached out her hand weakly to touch mine, but instead encountered the white tulip that I had

placed on her pillow. She studied it closely for some
time and the slightest smile seemed to form on her
mouth before she slowly drew the flower towards her
lips and made as if to kiss it.

For some time she remained quite still and I thought
that she had fallen into real sleep; but when I tried to
take the tulip from her in order to put it into a vase on
the bedside table, her fingers closed tightly about the
green stem and with her other hand she cupped the
bloom against her face as a woman does with the head
of her child.

She will move in the night and crush it, I thought,
and in the morning will regret it. But there was nothing
I could do. I kissed her quickly on the forehead, which
was cold and damp, and picking up the candle I left the
room.

I tapped gently on the door to Bella's room. She
opened it at once and by the light of the candle I could
see the eagerness in her eyes. She stretched out her
hand and I placed in it the small brown package that I
had collected from the town. She smiled briefly and
closed the door.

Further along the corridor I stopped outside the door
to Nina's room. There was no sound from within and I
waited for several minutes holding the candle and the
black tulip, uncertain as to whether I wanted to knock
on the door or not, unsure of what I felt, how tired I
was, how much in need of solitude. But before I had
finally made my mind up the door opened quietly and
without a word she came out onto the landing and half
pulled, half guided me into the room. She took the

flower and the candle and put them on a table and she pulled her nightdress off over her head and got into bed; the bedclothes were folded back and she waited, smiling, for me to get undressed and get in with her.

Even as I slowly undressed I had my doubts; certainly I felt desire, the warm bed, the wonderful warmth and pleasure that her body gave; yet at the same time I questioned my motives, a doubt mingled with a sense of hopelessness. I yielded again, I supposed, because I could not recall the good reason why I should refrain.

When we had made love she began to talk as usual about her preoccupations; about the house, food, or the state of the river that always worried her; sometimes she talked of her childhood in the town. Making love to Nina was a desperate, noisy, exuberant affair and I was quite sure that there was nothing feigned about her expression of pleasure. But once it was done she very quickly resumed an animated dialogue, though even this was in reality a monologue, an almost endless chatter that she would punctuate from time to time by clutching and squeezing me tightly against her. It was a gesture of companionship perhaps, or of sisterly affection and I liked it and drew strength and solace from it; but in the end she was a friend, sometimes intimate, and I looked elsewhere for a real lover.

Having just squeezed me violently she broke into her previous train of thought to ask me if I had delivered the drugs to Bella; I replied that I had. After a moment's silence she continued in a much sterner tone of voice, warning me that I had better not seek favors from Bella. Nina was suddenly very serious, and then silent, so that I gained the impression that she had mentioned something that she should not have. She shuddered in the bed beside me. I was aware that she was alluding to the fact that I might be tempted to try to make love to Bella. I questioned her half jokingly about what she had meant by her warning, but she would reveal no more except to say that if I would look in the top drawer of Bella's dressing table I would find a purple bag tied with a golden string.

We lay there for perhaps another hour and at times I dozed, then woke again to hear her still talking, slowly and quietly, partly to herself and partly to me. Eventually she fell asleep and I got up and dressed as silently as I could. I took the candle and left the room.

As I passed Bella's room I stopped, put the remaining flowers on a landing table, and listened at her door. There was no sound. I turned the handle and quickly stepped inside, closing the door silently behind me. She was naked and spread eagled upon a pile of cushions on the floor; she had been put into a deep sleep by the drugs. I moved closer to her, and stood over her, admiring almost objectively every detail of her body—the long slender limbs, the wonderful tension in the torso, the fineness of the fingers and toes and ears and breasts. Turning towards her dressing table, I paused a moment, convinced that she would not wake, yet in fear nevertheless. I turned back to look at her, but apart from a shallow breathing there was no movement in her body. I pulled the cover from the bed and lay it over her, partly to prevent her becoming cold, partly, as it were, to avoid being watched by her nakedness.

As I pulled open the top drawer I saw at once the purple bag, quite small and drawn closed with a golden cord. I opened it and let a heavy metal object roll into the palm of my hand. It was a beautiful polished silver orb, about two inches in diameter, with small, finely made wing-like structures protruding from the side. Slightly less than half the orb had been cut away and the interior was hollow except for a spear of metal, pointed and very sharp that was contained within the orb itself and did not protrude beyond its circumference. Attached to one side of the orb was a long, very fine, crimson thread. As I turned this in my hands and thought of what Nina had said to me, it gradually began to dawn on me what this object was. I shuddered and at once replaced it in its bag and closed the drawer.

I was anxious to leave the room but at the door I turned and went back to where she was lying. I pulled back the bed cover. A red thread was just visible at the top of her thigh. Very gently, hardly daring to breath, and while watching her face for signs of life, I pulled on the thread. I pulled very slowly until all resistance ceased, and then I looked down. There, couched at the edge of her vulva in the dark hair, was the glistening silver orb. For some time I simply stared at it, at the terrible beauty of it. Then I covered her again and quickly went out of the room.

For half an hour I sat in the dark on the landing, disturbed by what I had seen, worried by what she might conclude on waking; aware that since I was the only man in the house, that this device must have been used with me in mind. I felt I could understand her anxiety and fear, but it was difficult to accept the nature and form of her vengeance. But on the other hand, perhaps this was no more than a form of psychic protection like a spell or charm.

I was too tired, too confused to make sense of the situation; I knew only that she wore this thing, perhaps for every moment of her life; and I knew also that she chanted and prayed in the chapel, that she was an addict, crazy and dangerous.

Hardly aware of what I was doing I wandered into the room that was shared by Elena and Genia and found, as I had expected, that Elena's bed was still empty. I sat on Genia's bed and calmed and reassured her as she woke; I stroked her forehead, pushed back the hair from her eyes. As I had hoped, as I knew, the child was delighted with the purple tulip and thought it beautiful. She leapt from her bed and immediately fetched a jar of water to put it in. When she had positioned it precisely on her bedside table and admired it once more, she flung her arms around my neck to thank me. She got back into bed and I pushed the sheets in close under her chin, and gazing at the tulip that glowed naturally and simply in the candle-light, I began to tell her that I had also given a white tulip to Rebecca and that tomorrow she could visit her to see it; but when I turned to look down at her again her eyes were closed and she was sleeping.

Realizing that it was now the middle of the night, I crept downstairs as quietly as I could, knowing that I would have to pass Maria's door and that though she snored loudly she was also easily woken. In fact, to my surprise, her door was wide open and there was a candle burning inside the room. As I passed she called out to me.

"Thomas, I want to talk to you. I know it is late, but what I have to say is important."

As I entered the room she indicated with a gesture of her hand that I should sit in the chair at the foot of the large bed. She was half sitting up in bed against a mound of pillows, the palms of her hands face down on the counterpane. Her nightdress did not conceal her immense bosom. Her dark hair was let down and it flowed outwards and over her shoulders. She presented a strange image; an old woman, but painted, gaudy, obscene. But it was only after I had observed all this that I noticed that Frieda was sitting in a chair by the head of the bed and that she was staring at me intently.

"I have had a dream," Maria said slowly, "and it concerns you."

Before continuing she turned to Frieda and mumbled something whereupon Frieda got up and moved the candle so that it was no longer shining directly into my face. She then returned to her chair in the shadows.

In normal circumstances it would have been difficult for me to take this situation seriously, Maria holding court, the matriarchal oracle; but the presence of the silent Frieda changed that perception completely. Something important had occurred and I was alert, ready to give them my full attention.

Maria continued slowly, fixing me with her eyes that seemed almost lost in the fat wrinkles of her face. Her tone of voice was strident, unbearable, as if she admonished me for some trivial offense or misdemeanor and was determined that I should stay to experience the full, repetitive lashing of her thick red tongue.

"In the dream, which was exceptionally vivid and powerful, a strange and unnatural liaison occurred between a huntress and a wolf; these two, though enemies, made a pact in order to trap and destroy another much smaller animal. It seemed to me that this smaller animal was something like a mink and they wanted to kill it because it moved in the long grass and amongst the trees unseen, and with great cunning; and by so doing it alerted other game to the approach of both the huntress and the wolf.

"So together they tethered a blind doe by the fetlock in a clearing in the forest and waited in hiding. But when the mink tried to release the doe, the wolf broke cover too soon and in the confusion was shot by the huntress. The mink escaped, and the doe, panicked and terrified, blundered into the trees until it finally disappeared into the depths of the forest, never to be seen again.

The wolf bled and bled from its wound until it expired and was at last harmless."

Maria paused, still studying my face carefully as if she wanted me to absorb thoroughly the substance of her dream. But I realized immediately that whatever the dream might actually mean, it was at that moment of little importance compared to the interpretation that she had decided to impose on it. It was this interpretation which guided and formed her present feelings and which made her wait up so late to catch me as I descended the stairs.

"Obviously, Thomas," she began again, "if I am to accept that the dream refers to us in this house, as I must, then I can only assume that the blind doe represents Christina; that the small animal that tries to rescue her is, of course, Genia. And that the wolf who would attack them both, and who dies so slowly and painfully, is yourself."

"And the huntress." I asked. "Who is the huntress?"

"Only you Thomas know what liaisons you have made; only you know who might rely on your help."

For a moment I was silent, trying to understand what she was saying. I turned towards Frieda, still sitting silently in the corner by the head of the bed.

"And you Frieda, do you agree with the interpretation that Maria has made?"

I sensed rather than saw Frieda move as if to reply, as if to give an answer that was more subtle than simply yes or no. But before she could say anything Maria had spoken again.

"Frieda agrees that mine is the only possible interpretation. But I wonder Thomas, if you realize the danger that you are in. How easy it may be for you to be tempted. How essential it is that we give protection to the small and weak and innocent and blind, to all our children. But whatever transpires, Thomas, I sense that the huntress will sooner or later turn her gun on you and that unless you are careful, ever alert, ever listening, ever attentive and vigilant, that you will be unable to evade the bullet. You will die, Thomas, slowly and in pain, the thick stream of your blood pouring slowly from you, exactly as I have dreamt it..."

As she spoke the last few words, she leaned forward towards me as if to emphasize her meaning and her ancient, ugly face seemed to twist and leer; and I too leaned forward in my chair, transfixed by the stare of this old hag, and shocked into silence by the terrible interpretation that she placed upon her dream.

I could feel and think nothing except that this woman filled me with a sense of repulsion. I could imagine the gray mass of her brain and I could see the gross weight of her breasts and conjure up an image of her fat, sweating genitals; it was as if I was drawn towards her, as if she might embrace me and put me to her breast and crush me against her stinking body. It was vital that I fight with all my energy to get free of this woman, to escape into the open air, to free myself from her stifling clutches, to breath...

But though it seemed such a matter of life and death, for some time I could not move. I remained staring at her and breathing deeply, knowing that she had no inkling of the debauched thoughts that ran through my mind.

"I shall heed your warning," I said, and at last I got up from my chair and turned quickly and left the room.

On the landing I remembered the yellow rose that I had intended to give to Christina and hastily gathered it up and took it to my room and put it in water. I stripped off my clothes and took a long, cleansing and reviving shower.

I dressed warmly and went out into the night. It had stopped raining and the wind had died down somewhat, but the air was cold and damp and the moon invisible behind the clouds.

I walked out through the columns that supported the balcony and across the boulder-strewn area that separated the house from the sand bar. I walked on beyond this and onto the end of the rickety wooden jetty, where I sat down. The water, black and thick, swirled silently

around the flimsy supports and it seemed to me that the
river could so easily have swept it away. From where I
sat I could not see the house nor, of course, the far
shore so that it felt as if I floated at the mercy of the vast
surge of the river; sometimes I allowed myself to drift
with the flow, sometimes I was still; and sometimes via
an act of mental and visual trickery I could skim
upstream against the force.

As my anger subsided I began to consider what
Maria had said. She left me in no doubt of her certainty
that my life was threatened, that someone in the house
intended to kill me. And even if the dream had been a
fabrication, or the interpretation totally erroneous, nevertheless she had spoken in the end with such viciousness, such obvious relish for the substance of the dream,
that I had to believe that even if fate was not against me,
then this cruel and powerful woman wished to see me
destroyed. As I thought these things the shadow of a
night bird passed over me and frightened me, making
me realize how fearful I had become.

Feeling vulnerable to attack on the jetty, I got up and
almost ran back to the river's edge. I continued walking
quickly until I reached the small cove just up river from
the house where the old rowing boats had, years before,
been pulled up onto the sand. Massive magnetic boulders brought down the river by past floods surrounded
the cove and glowed in the strange deflected moonlight.
Some had been cracked open to reveal veins of brilliant,
luminous color.

This place held so many memories; of Christina
painting and of Christina swimming; of the bright green
weed; and, of course, of the water as it had been; crystal

clear in the sunlight, beautiful, drinkable, tangible...

It was then that I became aware of my reason for being so enraged by Maria's declarations. It was because she had dared to suggest that I might harm Christina; and worse, that Christina would be terrified and panicked and forced to flee. And though I felt that I could remain awake and alert and use all my cunning and strength to thwart the threat against myself, I did not know how I could also protect Christina who lived under the sway of the old woman; how could I watch over her, both by day and by night? It was impossible. The evil was in the house, and it seemed that there was little or nothing that I could do about it.

As I walked back towards my room I realized what a change had been wrought within me since the previous evening when I sat with them in the darkness of the balcony room. Then I had felt myself to be on the very edge of the household, essentially unimportant, unnoticed, able to go about my duties and live my private life. But now suddenly I was drawn onto the center stage, a light shone upon me and picked me out; I could no longer hide.

And whereas before Christina had been loved and desired at a distance, silently, and therefore without responsibility or commitment, now I found myself the key player in a mysterious game that could harm her; and only by taking action, by changing my relationship with her, by confronting her with my feelings would I be able to put myself in a position to offer her even minimal protection. I was deeply unsure that I was ready to make such a move.

As I lay face down on my bed and tried to sleep, my brain was assailed with images, not of Christina, but of Elena, her lover and my rival therefore. She paraded before me in all the costumes of the circus; and when I could no longer make the effort to fight off these images I let them smother and envelop me so that I fucked her this way and that, dressed and half-dressed, and finally on the sand in the center of the ring in the empty, soundless space. I lay there with her, too tired to move, until at last she simply melted away and was nothing.

I wondered why I so desired Elena whom I resented and disliked; and I wondered why my own mind worked against me in this way. There was only one simple answer; sexual intercourse was an act of aggression. Therefore I had just raped her, and serve the bitch right.

But with Nina, what did I feel? With Nina I took what I sometimes needed and would touch nothing else; a kind of endless theft. My detachment, it seemed, was complete, the very strongest of my possessions.

With Frieda whom I admired, I did not speak and nor did I really listen. With Genia I kept my distance, watching. And though a day did not pass in which I was not aware of Rebecca in her bed in the sick-room, nevertheless I would not allow her the status of a woman who needed love and care and attention; instead I remembered, and then waited until I had forgotten her, and so the latent feeling was lost.

Even the fear that Bella inspired in me was too much for me to bear, and I took it like a dead bird and hung it back around her own neck and pushed her back inside her room, her world, and shut the door on her.

But even if I should choose, was it really within my power to change the situation; or was it, as I suspected, that I was bewitched, rendered helpless, a victim of their collective spell. If this was true then I only needed simply and directly to restate my plan; one day I would pack up my few possessions and leave the house.

Three

I sat at the kitchen table drinking coffee and watching Nina as she prepared the breakfast trays for Frieda and Maria. I asked her about the weather and having considered the matter a few moments she replied that she thought it would become much colder. This suited me well. And in any case I had decided that my best occupation for that day would be to get in more wood for the fires.

As I was leaving the kitchen I stood behind Nina as she worked and placing my hands on her shoulders, I kissed her on the nape of the neck. She seemed surprised by this gesture, and as I left the house I wondered what my motive had been. But it was immediately clear to me; I needed an ally in the house, someone on whom I could rely to be my eyes and ears, to warn me of danger, and Nina was the only person who could fulfil this role.

As I was clearing the frost from the windshield of the truck and warming up the engine, Elena appeared to tell me that she had an important meeting with Maria and she asked me if I would take Genia with me for the morning. I said that I would. About ten minutes later Genia came out well dressed against the cold, her face bright and smiling. She climbed up onto the open back of the truck and grasped the bar behind the cab and we set off.

There were various tracks that I had made through the scrub-land in the direction of the forest and I tried to drive them in succession in order to keep them free of vegetation. At about one mile from the house at the edge of the forest there was a log cabin, not in any way connected with the house I believed, but erected years before by the people who cleared the strip of forest all along this side of the river. In this cabin I kept the chain saw and all the other equipment necessary for the logging. It was also a place in which to shelter for a brief respite from the freezing wind in the winter, somewhere to make a small fire and to have a drink.

During the previous winter I had cut down four large trees quite close to the cabin and it was this timber that I now logged and took back to the house. As I worked, sawing and splitting small logs for the kitchen stove and the boiler, and larger logs for the fireplace in the balcony room, Genia explored and inspected the area around the felled trees and along the edge of the forest. It was important to keep a close eye on her since it would have been so easy for her to stray into the forest while following some small wild animal or searching for a particular plant. A mere hundred yards into the forest and it became difficult to detect the source of light which indicated the way back towards the scrub-land; and a voice calling in the forest echoed and re-echoed against the trees and gave no hint as to its source.

At about mid-morning the wind suddenly dropped and it began to snow, a few isolated flakes spiralling down, melting at once on my gloves and on the saw, but immediately settling onto the timber. Genia, obviously delighted that it was snowing, came and helped me to load the truck. When we had finished we went into the cabin and I lit a fire in the tiny grate and brewed some coffee. As I did this Genia quietly explored every inch of the place, going into the small bedroom, lifting the covers of the bed, opening the drawers in the old battered cupboard. We sat opposite each other before the fire, our hands clasped about our mugs of coffee. I was looking at her, but the noise of the chain saw was still ringing in my ears, and I was thinking about the snow; that certainly before too long it would become heavier and begin to settle about the house. For how many days, I wondered, would it last. Genia was cold, she was shaking and her teeth were chattering, but she looked back at me smiling.

When I went to the window and cleaned away the mixture of cobwebs and dirt and condensation, I saw that the snow was beginning to obscure the track; I knew that we must not be too long before we left. Already it was difficult to make out the house.

At that moment Genia came and stood behind me, encircling me with her arms and laying her head against my back. Because of the thickness of our clothing the embrace had the innocence of a bear hug and I thought that if I turned within the circle of her arms to face her,

she would laugh and release me. But she sensed that I
was about to turn and she held me more tightly so that I
could not move. When she spoke her voice was muffled, her mouth buried deep in the material of my coat.

"Thomas, will you let me see you?"

"See me?" I had no idea what she meant.

"Naked."

As I looked from the window I was aware that the situation was changing rapidly; there was a blizzard blowing, and it therefore became important that I got the
load of logs back to the house as quickly as possible in
order to try to return for another load before it was too
late. At the same time that I was aware of this urgency, I
also wanted to be able to turn to face her, to put my
hand on her hair perhaps, and to stroke it gently.

"It is not possible." I said. "Particularly at this time. It
is not possible for reasons that I an unable to explain."

"But Thomas, I see Elena all the time; and Christina
too. But I have only seen photographs of statues of men,
and drawings. How will I ever see a man?"

"I think that Nina may have some photographs that
would be better. I will speak to her." I spoke the words
coldly, irritated and angry that my inevitable response
to her request would offend her deeply and that our
friendship would be spoilt. It had, no doubt, been difficult to ask me and now, in a sense, I had betrayed her.
The request was simple, almost beautiful in its simplicity; yet it was unanswerable in that house at that time.

Without talking and without looking at each other we
put out the fire and left the cabin. In spite of the snow,
she insisted on riding on the back of the truck again, this
time standing precariously astride the pile of logs.

I drove slowly, ensuring that I did not stray too far off the track. At about half way to the house there was a loud banging on the cab roof and I stopped the truck. She climbed down from the back and got into the cab beside me, slamming the heavy door. She asked me to switch off the engine, which I did.

"Thomas." But she spoke my name while breathing hard, and when she spoke it next it was a calm, enticing sound. "Thomas, perhaps I did not make myself clear. I meant to say that you could also see me. And that you could touch me. If you wanted."

"And who tells you that I might want to touch you? Maria? Elena?"

"Yes."

"But not Christina?"

"Christina is your friend. Christina loves you."

"So this touching would be a bad thing, would it; a wrong thing?"

"Not with us, Thomas. It would not be wrong between us, would it?"

And she looked at me, her brown eyes wide open; her small hand moved onto the back of my gloved hand and her fingers spread and tried to grasp it.

The snow began to build up on the windshield and the light inside the cab was soft and intimate. We moved closer on the seat and I put my arm around her. At first I stroked her hair and kissed her forehead, then her cheek which was cool and unbelievably tender. She lifted her lips to mine, and her fine eyes questioned, and her small cold hand with its golden rings moved, softly......

No, not so.

I cursed Elena, and longed desperately for my beloved Christina, and cursed again the great brown eyes that were fixed upon me; casually I flicked her hand off mine.

"Pig." She screamed at me. "Pig, pig, pig."

She leapt from the cab slamming the door behind her, and began to trudge off into the blizzard. I leaned over and pushed the door open again and shouted after her to come back, not to be so damn stupid. But I had to get out and run after her, physically stop her, get her firmly in my arms until she stopped fighting and kicking; and then I bundled her back in the cab and started the engine. But before I drove off I told her, almost shouting at her, that she had to try to understand my feelings; but her stubborn, furious expression did not alter and she did not reply.

Later I suggested more quietly that at the house we should go to the kitchen and drink a warming brandy together. But she simply told me to go to hell.

Fantasy became reality and reality became fantasy. It did not matter which was which. I lived the reality for a moment in time, and the fantasy from year to year; the sense of regret and loss was the same. Both separated me from a sensation, a feeling, the beginnings of a feeling that might have been greater than both. But in the end the process of living was merely painful, an endless, indeterminate ache; and the recollection of the life being lived was a kind of death.

When I had unloaded and stacked the logs at the back of the house, I went to the kitchen and sipped at a brandy while I sat at the kitchen table. Nina worked around me, but did not say a word. When I had suffi-

ciently improved my state of mind I went upstairs to the
studio. Christina was alone and asked me to come in at
once and seemed pleased to see me.

She was as usual sitting at a small table and working
at one of the clay heads. And as usual I placed my hand
lightly and quickly on her shoulder by way of greeting. I
knew that she did not like to be watched, especially
when she was working, so I went at once and sat near to
the window. But between the two large windows there
was a mirror on wheels and I quietly positioned this so
that she would sense that I was looking and talking
away from her, though I was in fact able to watch her as
she worked. '

She held her head close to the clay, occasionally
pushing her fair hair off her face with the back of her
hand. To maneuver the clay she used her fingers and
palms combined with a short piece of wood flattened at
the end. It was only occasionally when she flung her
head back to face the ceiling while at the same time her
hands continued to work, that it was possible to detect
that she was blind.

I told her that it was snowing, but she said that Elena
had already told her earlier on. I asked her if she knew
why Elena had been summoned to see Maria, and she
replied that she thought it was something to do with a
dream. I told her that I had been sawing logs near to the
forest, that according to Nina the cold weather was here
to stay, and that I hoped to get in more logs before the
day was out. I spoke slowly, not concentrating on what I
was saying, because I was watching her intently. As often
occurred in her presence, I entered a sort of trance, an
intense daydream, in which I silently itemized what I

was seeing and experiencing, and sometimes I know that my lips moved as I heard the words in my mind: calm, serene, beautiful, gentle, artist, perfect, perfection, (I love you), female, feminine, femininity, girl, tragic, woman, blind, grace, perfection......and so on, watching her in the mirror until I had to stop; to stop, to wake up before I drove myself mad.

So at last I turned my eyes away from the mirror towards the window and the view beyond.

"Thomas, you said that you wanted me to give you lessons, but you have not come to me in the early evenings as I suggested. It seems to me that it would be such a good idea and I would love to teach you, and I am sure that you would benefit; you could make anything you wished, anything at all, and see what happened, see what you thought; and we could help each other with difficult pieces, and advise each other. And if you felt that you had to repay me, then of course there are a hundred jobs here in the studio which you could easily manage..."

But I was not listening. I had to admit that sometimes her conversation, her monologue, suggested an unreality; it was sometimes slight and almost fey. And that, no doubt, was because she could not see.

Instead I was looking from the window, with its view over the vast spread of the river. In the distance the brown of the river formed a pediment to the falling snow, but closer to me I could see that their movements were opposed; the river without cease flowing horizontally to the west, and the snow slanting down from the other direction and seeming to vanish before it actually touched the surface of the water. It seemed a continuous movement that would never end.

I got up and stood behind her chair in order to catch a brief glimpse of her sculpture before I left. I realized then that she was modelling the head of Elena, and I breathed her name.

"Good." She said. "Is it really like her? Like her in spirit, I mean?"

I mumbled that it was, that it was quite brilliant, and I asked how she could achieve such a likeness. At once she wiped her hands and asked me to kneel down before her. Her fingers were cold and smooth from the clay and as she moved them over my face she named the parts she touched.

"Eyes, eye-lashes, bridge of nose, eye-brows, forehead, hair-line, ears, cheeks, nose, nostrils, upper lip, lower lip, chin, jaw-bone, neck, the whole of the neck, the back of the head, the whole of the head..."

And as her fingers explored, so my head dropped naturally towards her lap. I rested my head there for some time, and her fingers became still. When finally I raised my head I saw that her eyes were directed far across the room. Very slightly and slowly her lips moved. I was convinced that she was recalling memories, memories from her youth. Quietly I got up from my knees and sat in a chair close to her; for the first time I began a close and minute study of her eyes.

Her eyes; the shape and color and texture as she remembered; the way in which they moved suddenly as if startled, or darted away from something unpleasant; and lingered, paused longingly over an image that gave comfort and pleasure.

And I too began to remember; the eternal, ethereal passion that I had once planned with her, a marriage of minds, a love sanctioned by the gods; a love in which silence, the night, the moon, one hand clasping another, watching her walk, watching her sleep, letting my finger run within the small white shell of her ear, all these things would give rise to an overwhelming ecstasy that would banish the need for every other thing.

This dream, if it was a dream, had not changed, had not evolved naturally into something else, but had been brutally and systematically destroyed. But what had brought about a destruction so total that all that remained was a wine-sodden moment with a photograph in the dark of a dingy café. Was it the pollution, the loss of the pure shining water, and the loss of her sight? Or was that in itself no more than a symptom of the actual disease? Had I allowed the feelings and hopes to slip away from me little by little in my bravura quest for appearance; so that now my face was a mask, and my body was skin and bone armored against itself.

Without moving her eyes from their fixed position she began to talk rapidly and her tone was agitated and fearful.

"Thomas, you must help me. Sometimes I am so frightened. You must protect me. I feel that they will destroy me if they can. You must come to me..." And she stretched out her hands suddenly in my direction and I would have leapt to my feet and caught hold of them but at that moment the door was flung open and Elena moved quickly into the room.

Christina knew immediately who it was and her tone of voice changed at once.

"Is Genia with you?" she asked.

"No, she is with Maria. I came to see if you needed anything."

Elena's voice was hard; she fixed her eyes on me
with an intense and suspicious stare.

"Maria has suggested that we re-organize your room to
make it better for you. Bring the bed out of the corner."

"But the room is perfectly well arranged," I said, hor-
rified by this suggestion. "And in any case Christina
knows her way about it as it is."

But Christina spoke quickly. "No, no, Thomas, I
think it could be re-organized a little. That would be
good. I am grateful. Maria is so good at these things."

Conditions were getting worse, the snow settling
deeply and drifting; because there was an urgent need
to get in more wood, Nina agreed to help me. We drove
back out to the cabin where we worked together very
quickly and efficiently; while I sawed, she positioned
the lengths of timber. When we had finished and loaded
the truck, Nina went into the cabin to light a fire while I
gathered together the equipment.

I knew that between us on these occasions there was
an understanding, a kind of pact, and I was not surprised when I went inside to find her half sitting up on
the bed, her skirt pulled up around her waist. Her eyes
were closed, but she could neither prevent nor hide the
strange smile that flitted about her mouth. I knelt
between her thighs and spent a long time touching her;
and when I was in her I unfastened the buttons at the
top of her dress and pulled up the vest that she was
wearing and exposed to my gaze and to my touch her
beautiful breasts.

After a while she insisted that we get fully undressed
and go out into the snow. And there we rolled around

and laughed and played all the stupid games that we always played. I rubbed snow onto her breasts and she screamed with the cold and with the pleasure of it, and mouthed oaths at me for coming out of her to do random body prints in the snow, before entering the warmth of her again with renewed and glorious pleasure.

In the cabin we put our clothes back on in silence. When she had dressed she picked up a rusty shot gun from the corner of the room and pretended to shoot me with it. I told her that I always had the intention of throwing the thing in the river, but always forgot. She said then that there was a gun of some sort in the house, but when I asked her where, she could not remember; in Maria's room perhaps, because she seemed to remember seeing Genia playing with it. I asked her to tell me if she saw it again.

As we drove slowly back to the house Nina was silent; and I was preoccupied with memories of that morning, of Genia riding on the pile of logs, of her hand resting in mine.

That evening during dinner I noticed the red bruise low on Nina's neck where my teeth had marked her and it seemed to me that she made a point of showing it off to Genia and Maria. It would have been so easy for her to have worn something that would have covered the mark, but obviously she had purposely not done so. It was odd that she wished to annoy me. I felt a curious, unsettling sense of betrayal.

After the evening meal when music was being played on the gramophone, Frieda and I decided to retire to her room to complete a game of chess that we had begun some time before. Her room was a strange, exotic sanctuary, a lair where she spent most of her life. The room was quite dark, the heavy curtains always half closed, and the paint work mostly brown. The furniture was also dark and heavy, and likewise her bed was a massive oak four-poster with an old, faded gray canopy. The walls were lined with books, mostly old and leather bound. There were several tables arranged in a dense mass at the center of the room and at all four sides of this arrangement there was a solid upright chair with wooden arms. Heaped on these tables were piles of manuscripts, each covered in thousands of minutely penned ideograms or hieroglyphs, it was difficult to tell which; and it was also dangerous to inspect them too closely since between all the piles and sometimes lurking under the covers of books were dozens of mousetraps, all baited and set. It was the task of translation or interpretation that occupied Frieda's days and often her nights.

We sat at a small table at the foot of the bed and I set up the chess pieces. She produced, as she usually did, two small glasses and an unlabelled bottle containing a delicious brown nectar which was presumably brandy, but with the addition of something else. As we sipped this in silence, we slowly played the game.

Occasionally as I waited for her to make her move I gazed about the room; some of the shelves in the center of the bookcases were free of books and displayed instead small objects, totems, animals, pieces of carved stone from the ancient world. By the bed was a lectern on which a large leather bound book was open; this also was composed of hieroglyphs.

She did not like to talk while playing chess, but afterwards as we sat quietly drinking the brandy, I wanted to ask her about these manuscripts, what they were, where from, and what knowledge she gained from them. But at that moment she seemed to sense that I was about to enquire, and her wrinkled hands stiffened on the arms of her chair; the line of her mouth became more taut, and she seemed to toss her head very slightly and to give a short sniff as if to warn me away from an area that was private and secret. But one day I would ask her. I would not be put off forever. One day when I felt calm enough to listen, then I would hear all that she had to say.

She had a way of fumbling with the brooch on her dress to indicate that she wanted to be alone. I got up from my chair at once and thanked her for the drink. As I put my hand on the door handle she called out to me and stopped me; when I turned she looked me directly in the eyes.

"I do not want you to be frightened, Thomas," she said. "I know that you are strong. But you must be vigilant, at all times vigilant. They want to deceive you, but you must see clearly; you must see the truth and not turn away. Do you understand what I am saying?"

I replied that I understood and she opened the door for me and closed it quietly behind me. In fact all that I understood was that I was being warned of danger, but of the form it would take I had no idea. But as I stood on the landing outside her door, I was disturbed mostly by the hint of desperation that had been in her voice. Frieda, who was normally so calm, so contained, was nervous and alarmed.

On the following morning it had stopped snowing,
though it lay deep about the house. As I was stacking logs
in the recesses at each side of the fireplace in the balcony
room, I saw and heard Maria and Elena and Genia playing outside the windows in the snow on the balcony.

They had made a snow man and were hurling snow
balls at each other; I heard Genia's high-pitched laugh
and the deeper tones of Maria's voice. I saw Genia's
slight figure, first at one window and then at another as
she ran round and round, gathering up the snow and
hurling it in every direction.

When I returned a little while later with more logs I
noticed that Elena was sitting on the parapet, seeming
to be deep in thought as if she had suddenly decided
not to join in with the game. But as I watched she fell
suddenly forward as if unconscious and collapsed heavily into the snow. I ran at once to the window and flung
it open and went out in her direction to lift her, convinced that she had fainted because of the cold, or else
that she was ill. But as I approached Maria warned me
to keep away, telling me that everything was under control and that she could manage. The old woman sat on
the parapet and with great difficulty managed to heave
Elena's body onto her lap. She began to slap her face in
a futile attempt to revive her. Genia stood nearby, still
holding a snowball in her hands. Maria again told me
that all was well and that I should go back inside; and
so, reluctantly I obeyed.

As I closed the window I turned to look at the
strange group; the black haired old woman in her black
coat with the slender body of the young woman arched
uncomfortably across her lap, the face white, the mouth

open, the eyes still tight shut; and the child, interrupted in its play, hovering, upset and anxious. And as I watched, Maria put her free arm around Genia's shoulder and drew her in closer, and as she did so Maria raised her head and stared straight ahead of her, a look of mad triumph on her face. Like a dog that is starved, she had instantly turned the situation to her advantage in order to experience a fleeting moment of crude ecstasy; this pathetic tableau, this pieta... with which she used and abused the two young women.

But even as I watched Maria's strength waned and she let Elena's still lifeless body fall awkwardly from her lap into the snow. At once I heard her order Genia to fetch me, but I was already there, lifting Elena. And as I carried her back into the room, I was amazed at how light she was; indeed it was a miracle, because she seemed to have no weight at all but to be merely a sensation of touch in my arms.

When I reached the balcony room door, with Maria and Genia running in my wake, Maria told me to take her straight into her room on the same floor. But before I could get through the door, Elena opened her eyes and finding herself being carried, she seemed suddenly to panic; she screamed to be put down. I continued until I reached Maria's bed but even as I laid her down gently she screamed again to be released and left alone. Maria ushered me from the room and slammed the door in my face; for some time afterwards as I stood outside I could hear the screaming continuing, and hear Maria's useless attempts to comfort and calm her.

As I prowled the house that night, alert to all strange sounds, I heard a noise in Maria's room as if someone was fumbling endlessly with the door handle. As I opened it cautiously I saw Elena dressed in her night-gown on her knees just inside the door. She looked exhausted and looked at me desperately and asked where Maria was. I replied that I assumed that in order not to disturb her and to allow her to rest, she had gone to sleep in Elena's own bed in the room with Genia. At once she began to moan and to sway from side to side as if in the grip of some awful spasm. She tried to get to her feet, but fell back. I helped her to bed, but as she lay there trying to catch her breath, she pleaded with me to help her reach her own room.

She leaned against me, and without touching her more than was absolutely necessary, I guided her along the corridor and up the flight of stairs. But the door to her room was locked on the inside. At once she demanded almost hysterically that I break it down. I called out to Maria, and then to Genia, but there was no reply; and I hammered as hard as I could, still calling their names, until I became convinced that something must be wrong. I ran outside to the back of the house as fast as I could and returned with the axe and smashed a hole near to the door handle. I put my hand through, turned the key and threw open the door.

The far bed, which was Elena's, was empty, but in the near one cowered the enormous bulk of Maria, lying on her side and half turned towards me, her head lifted and her eyes blazing. Elena immediately shouted for Genia; and then, as Maria began to lift herself, I saw beneath her the curled body of Genia, her arms about her head, her eyes closed and her small body shaking with terror.

I helped Elena to her own bed, and then carefully lifted Genia and placed her in with her. As they clung to each other, Maria got up and stood in the center of the room, her nightgown reaching almost to her feet; her black hair, untied, framing her fat face as she blustered on about believing that she was being attacked and wanting to defend the child. I waited by the door until she had left the room and I waited on the landing until I heard her close the door to her room on the floor below.

Turning back into the room, I looked at Elena and Genia curled in each other's arms. Elena, it seemed to me, looked in my direction as she stroked Genia's hair and tried to calm her. I could have said something, I wanted to say something; but I did not. I pulled the battered door on them and returned to my room.

Lying on my bed, unable to sleep, I was not surprised to find my thoughts returning again and again to Elena; and soon the familiar fantasy began to fill my mind. She was the bare-backed rider and her horse galloped in the ring; but this time as she began the leap onto its back, she fell. I rushed forward from my seat to lift her up, but she was not hurt and she was weightless in my arms; and I kissed her as if I loved her...

The fantasy was spoilt, contaminated by the events of the evening, effectively destroyed because I had had actual physical contact with her, had felt her body within my arms, felt its warmth and lightness. But I could not sleep and again the fantasy came and again it failed, failed as I lifted her and kissed her like a lover.

For perhaps an hour or two I dozed. I awoke for some reason, aware that it was snowing again. I was

cold. I had momentarily forgotten the events of the previous evening and as I lay quite still the fantasy returned
and she leapt upon the horse and she did not fall; and at
last I possessed her and pushed her down hard on the
sand in the center of the ring and stood up at peace and
closed my eyes and turned away and forgot her.

When I woke in the morning there was a moment's
regret, a sense almost that I might have been impatient,
committed a minor desecration. But I soon recalled old
memories that quickly banished these feelings; these
women were mad, all mad, and I was wise to keep my
distance and maintain my guard.

Four

I had never known such a cold winter. During the day there was no glimmer of sunlight and at night the temperature dropped well below zero so that the snow became deeper and the top layer froze into a hard crust. If the bad weather continued unabated I knew that it would become more and more difficult to bring in logs. I was uncertain at that time if it was already important to turn down the heating in order to save wood. It was also impossible to get to the town, and though there was a good supply of stand-by provisions, tins and dried foods etc., a decision still had to be made as to when we would start to ration ourselves. I would have to talk to Frieda, and consult with Nina. But an even more urgent consideration was to warn Bella that because I could no longer get to the town, she must try to make her drugs last as long as possible.

I began to search for her. She was not in her room, so I
went to the chapel.

The room, part of the old tower of the castle, was in
semi-darkness; two large candles burned on the table
that served as an altar. There were three small high windows, one containing remnants of stained glass, and
none of them admitting much light. The walls were of
bare stone, hung here and there with various pieces of
material and small tapestries, old and faded. There were
two rows of chairs on each side of a wide aisle, and the
large, carpeted space in front of the altar had two heavily carved chairs or thrones, one at each side. The altar
itself was draped in a simple white cloth. Issuing from
somewhere behind it there was the sound of music, a
repetitive percussive sound, increasing very gradually in
tempo and volume towards a crescendo. Bella, dressed
in a red robe, was seated on one of the thrones.

As I approached she raised her hand to halt me, but
she did not turn in her chair. I sat down at the back of
the room and waited. I was reluctant to interrupt her
during her service or meditation or whatever it was, but
at the same time I hoped that she would not keep me
waiting too long. I found the chapel unsettling and her
presence unnerving. Through the small leaded window
above the altar I could see the snow falling relentlessly;
and though the room was not cold, nevertheless I began
to shiver.

As my eyes grew accustomed to the light I noticed
all kinds of small objects on the altar, all arranged
neatly in a long row. Gradually I began to recognize
these things as the possessions of the others that had
either disappeared or that we knew her to have stolen

over the years. There was a silver comb belonging, I think, to Frieda, and Genia's brooch in the form of a lion, and Nina's silver ring with the pale blue stone. These and many other objects, all clean and shining and obviously treated with great reverence, adorned the altar. At the extreme end of the row there was a knife, really a hunter's knife that I kept in the truck and used for a multitude of odd purposes. I had assumed that it was lost. I saw it then shining in the flickering light from the candles, much brighter than it had ever been before.

As the drumming music increased in volume she approached the altar and picked up the first object and held it tight with both hands and brought it close against her body. At the same time she lifted her face as if looking at the light that came through the small window above the altar; and she began to chant, at first inaudibly, her lips hardly moving, and then louder so that I could hear that she spoke over and over again in quick succession the name of Frieda. And as she progressed from object to object and name to name so her manner became more intense, more fraught and her voice less controlled and louder, so that she hammered on the altar with a silver cup that belonged to Rebecca and beat it against her chest, as if a great anger and fury were rising within her.

Finally, she picked up the knife; with a sudden movement she held it high above her head, the blade pointing downwards. Then she turned quickly to face me and brought the knife down swiftly, and clutched it tight against her belly. For a brief moment she fixed me with her black eyes and began to chant my name, on and on, faster and faster. And she did not cease until long after the music had stopped and there was only her voice rising and falling, whispering and calling, a hellish dirge that was almost impossible to bear, yet at the same time was utterly compelling and hypnotic. At last she fell silent and collapsed slowly upon the carpet and the knife fell from her grasp. She lay still for some time; when she stirred she rose with a strange dignity, replaced the knife on the altar, and sat with great ceremony in one of the thrones. She beckoned me to sit in the one at the opposite corner of the altar, and this I did. When she spoke her voice was quiet and calm.

"You see, Thomas, that I pray for you all."

"And to what god do you pray?" I asked.

"To the river god and the forest god and the snow god and the moon god and the rain god and the sun god and the man god and the woman god and the white god and the black god..."

"And when you pray to these gods, what do you ask for?"

"I pray to guard you all against emptiness and to protect you all from the void, so that the innocence and joy of Genia will not be lost, nor the emotion and blood of Nina be destroyed, nor the wisdom and intuition of Frieda be dispersed to the four winds, nor the strength and vision of Elena be wasted, nor the purity and beauty of Christina be damaged; and I pray that Rebecca will not slide into death, I pray for her life and her sex."

"And Maria?" I said. "You have not mentioned Maria."

"You do not love Maria. How can I pray for her if you do not love her?"

"But how can I love her?" I asked. "How could it be possible?"

"You have made her ugly, but you must return her to a state of beauty; sooner or later, whatever the consequences, it must be done."

As I watched her I was impressed, no, rather I was moved by her stillness, her composure, the strength of the image in which only the dark lips moved and the pink tongue darted between the white teeth; the red of her robe, her wild black hair, the shining gold of her earrings and her rings, the black face and black hands and black feet perfectly still. No doubt the silver orb was within her, and certainly drugs ran in her veins, but I had not seen this strength in her before, nor heard this solemn voice.

I asked her what she prayed for precisely when she prayed for me.

"I pray, Thomas, that you will not betray us nor desert us. I pray that you will not sacrifice your soul; and I pray that you will not exchange your life for a useless fantasy, an everlasting round of delusion, deceit and escape; and I pray, of course, that you will come to know us."

"I know you well enough."

"No, Thomas, we have cried out to you, but you have not listened, nor yielded, nor received us into your being. Your attention has wandered, an aimless nomad lost in the barren desert, and you have tried to blame us for your daily torment. You give nothing, therefore you feel nothing."

For some time we sat in silence as I pondered the odd notion that this woman prayed for me in this way.

Yet her words were not without a strange power, and I felt myself drawn down into an abyss, a falling into confusion and pain, into an anarchic, dangerous world; a world that suggested meaningless torture, of blood rites and feuds and animal passion and instinct, from which there would be no escape, in which there would be no death.

Yet I was able to oppose these feelings; as I sat with her in the chapel my serenity came from the depths of my being, from the certainty that I would one day leave this house, abandon them all to their madness. There was no doubt in my mind that I would soon escape their clutches, and find my own world of sanity and order.

But I was curious to explore this unforeseen vein of solemnity in her, and I asked if she prayed for herself. For a moment she stared back at me and her eyes widened as if I had asked an illogical or stupid question.

But then she began to cry; her face retained its composure, but the tears poured down her face and over her closed lips. I stared back at her, fearing some trick, suddenly afraid of her again and unable to move.

"I pray for my baby, God's baby, our baby." She cried out, and coming towards me quickly she grasped my hand and thrust the palm against her belly. "Feel, Thomas, feel in there. Feel my baby."

But I felt only a taut, flat stomach.

"I feel nothing," I said, and at once she pulled away from my hand and flung herself at the altar, kneeling in front of it, her head in her hands. She began to weep again, her body heaving and sighing as she tried to stop the flood of tears.

Eventually she was able to speak.

"In the forest the sisters were suddenly attacked without warning by the people, the tribal people. But a temporary peace was made, an escape route guaranteed if one of us would go over as a hostage, a gift, a sacrifice. And I was chosen. The sisters drugged me, and when I woke I was in pain in my belly and I was bleeding. I was given more drugs for the pain. They told me that God would forgive me the rape, the violation, but that I must avoid the seed; I must not carry the devil within me.

"They left me in a clearing in the forest, but the village man who came to find me was my brightest pupil in the school, my best boy, and in a way I loved him. I could not let him touch me, could not let him rape me...

"I killed him. With a machete I hacked him to pieces. I escaped from the forest, guided by God. I heard that the sisters were massacred, one by one tracked down and killed.

"But God has forgiven me, and he has given me a child of his own. I, a virgin, have been given his child and it grows within me, little by little. And one day, Thomas, with your help it will grow big enough to be born. Feel Thomas, believe and feel..."

I knelt down behind her and placed my palm on her stomach again; my other hand I rested gently on her shoulder.

"Did a child die?" I asked. "Did your child die?"

"Children die all the time, Thomas. They die because they do not have sugar and water and salt, simple things. And their mothers sit in quiet agony and watch, unable to cry out, because they are aware in the depths of their souls that it has been this way since the beginning of time; and now it is no different. Without uttering a word we damn them and curse them and we do nothing to end their misery.

"But our child, Thomas, is the child of God and we will not let it die; we will cherish it and make it grow, and one day I will give birth and you will see that what I say is true, that it is a child of the new age, a new beginning, a new hope..."

Suddenly she fell away from me and lay on her back before the altar. Her eyes seemed to roll in her head, and though I knew it to be merely the effect of the drugs, nevertheless she resembled a witch, trapped in a devilish trance. I pitied her for her addiction; and I pitied her that she was so riven with delusions, so obsessed with longings that she could never hope to fulfil. But I could no more hear these confessions than I could be a partner in her crimes.

Quietly I told her what I had come to say, that she should not depend on me being able to get to the town to renew her supply of drugs. She replied that she did not need them anymore, that she was free of them, no longer dependent.

As I was about to leave the chapel she flung herself at my feet and begged me to feel her stomach once more, to feel the child within. When I refused she caught hold of my legs, restraining me, demanding to know if she had not been calm and answered all my questions and would I now deny her this last request. But I would not join her game, would not give credence to this dangerous and maudlin fantasy.

But she lunged at me again with tremendous force and dragged me to the ground, and her voice was crazed and violent.

"Feel, Thomas, it moves, it moves.... Feel."

And when she thrust my hand there it was true that I could feel a movement; a dull thud against the tight wall of her belly, once, and then repeated several times quickly, and then once again. She could see by my expression that I had felt it, and the tension went out of her body and she lay calmly and softly beside me; her eyes closed, and for the first time a faint smile came to her lips. I withdrew my hand and got up and left her alone in the chapel.

After dinner that evening I helped Nina clear the table and take the dishes back down to the kitchen. When I returned to the balcony room there was no one there; they had all retired to their rooms. I poured a flask of water on the fire, knowing that it would not really put it out, but I was reluctant to leave a blazing fire in an empty room. I took a bottle of wine and a glass, intending to go to my room to use music and wine to put myself into a long deep sleep.

As I passed the kitchen Nina accosted me, telling me that since the others had gone to bed, I must help her with Rebecca; she was due to have a bath and have clean sheets put on her bed and so on, and that she could not manage this by herself. I protested that it was not right that I should be involved in such things, but Nina would accept no excuses. From the linen cupboard she loaded me down with sheets and towels and a nightdress, and led the way to the sick-room.

The room was illuminated by a single, shaded lamp at Rebecca's bedside. She stirred as we entered and opened her eyes, and seemed to express some pleasure at seeing us. The white tulip had not been crushed but was in a slender glass vase by her bed. At once Nina began to talk to her, a non-stop stream of news and comment, telling her why we had come, what she had been doing, about Genia, about the depth of the snow, asking whether she had enjoyed the soup that night, and so on. Nina asked me to go to the bathroom to run a bath. When I returned to the room she had pulled the bedclothes right back and was swinging Rebecca's legs down onto the floor. Together we half carried, half walked her to the bathroom between us.

We sat her in a chair next to the bath and helping her to lean forward, Nina removed her nightgown. I was disturbed immediately by the sight of so much hair that grew on her shoulders and her back, hair like some men have, in random, unsightly tufts. But I was completely taken by surprise by the thick red hair that began at her pubic area and spread upwards onto her stomach and downwards onto the top of her thighs and on her legs; in the creases of her flesh its density was like that of an animal, and I was so shocked by this that I could only stare at her in horror. I looked at her sad, drained, ghostly face and I realized that she saw my dismay and repugnance. She took my hand and squeezed it with what little strength she had, as if to reassure me. But as she did this, I am sure her eyes appealed for mercy, begged me not to turn away.

Nina ordered me to work up a lather in a shaving bowl and then with me assisting as best I could, she shaved Rebecca's stomach, thighs, and legs. Though she was clearly very weak, she did her best to help us in the task. When we were finished we lowered her carefully into the bath and her pleasure at the contact with the warm water was obviously enormous. Nina and I returned to the bedroom to deal with the bed, but I stopped her, desperate for some explanation of Rebecca's illness. The illness, Nina said, was a kind of sleeping sickness and it was accompanied in Rebecca's case by a gradual decay of her femininity that needed to be constantly arrested, constantly fought against. It was this battle, this battle to survive as a woman that exhausted Rebecca and sapped her strength.

"And will the hair grow back?" I asked.

"Of course, in about a month; then I will shave it again."

"But what is the point, if it simply grows back again; surely it is painful to be shaved like that?"

"Thomas, you may be in ignorance of us, but surely you are aware in your own male life of the role that simple vanity plays in the growth of one's energies, one's courage to face the world, one's strength to live. She is a woman, Thomas; you must see that she is a woman, and treat her as a woman."

She asked me to go back to the bathroom and to wash Rebecca's hair. Using the shower spray as carefully as I could I began to wet the mass of coarse red hair, and then to work in the shampoo, and to gather the hair from her face and her neck and to move my fingers within it. Massaging her scalp, watching the soap run down over her shoulders and breasts into the bath water, I was drawn into a state of reverie, something to do with the bright lights of the bathroom, and something to do with the curious fact that as I continued I began to find her body attractive, warm and desirable. I searched in childhood memory for the occasion of a particular sensation not dissimilar to this; warmth, a deep and comforting satisfaction of some sort. Had I washed my mother's hair like this; or was there some other woman to whom I was close? I did not know, I could remember nothing. Finally I decided that my feeling of tenderness arose solely from a sense of pity for her.

When Rebecca was back in the bed, Nina asked me to sit by her and talk to her. I could think of little to say and so talked about the weather and about the logging which was obsessing me at that time. She seemed not to be listening, so I fell silent. But when Nina returned from the bathroom she chided me, telling me that Rebecca heard everything, and that I should try and talk about things that might interest her; Nina's expression was that Rebecca was "a woman deprived of life."

I talked about Christina, about her studio, her sculpture; and then because she seemed to have almost fallen asleep, and I too was desperately tired, I began a quiet meandering monologue about my feelings for Christina, and my fears for her safety, and my dreams for the future. When I fell silent I felt her hand near mine, and I felt her fingers grip mine as hard as they could.

When I looked at her, her eyes were open again and she was trying to say something. I leaned very close in order to hear what she said. I could smell her foul breath. She seemed to say "Kill Maria." but I could not be certain.

Nina returned, saying that it was time to let her sleep. I kissed Rebecca on her forehead and rose to leave.

At the door Nina turned on me, saying, "Kiss her, Thomas, kiss her properly."

Looking back at Rebecca I saw that her arms were outstretched towards me, and her head slightly raised as she waited and hoped and begged to be kissed. But I could not kiss her. I returned to the bed and avoiding her arms, kissed her again quickly on the forehead. She was breathing deeply and wheezing, her eyes shut and her arms still outstretched, but I could not bring myself to kiss her on the mouth.

As we went back down the stairs, I was fully aware that soon, tomorrow or in the near future, it would seem so easy to have kissed her; that I would regret the omission. Already I felt that I had made a mistake, a bad mistake; I had failed to act and I would always regret it. But worse than this; I felt certain that I had been given a chance there in the sick-room in the quiet of the night to alter subtly the course of my own destiny. But because the harmless, easy act was distasteful to me, I had let the chance slip away.

Five

When I returned to my room I could not sleep. The wind began to pick up again and was whistling through the columns that supported the balcony. I lay on the bed and listened to the wind. I was extremely cold and suspecting that the boiler had gone out, I went to look; but it was working perfectly well. Sitting on the edge of the bed draped in blankets, I was on the point of abandoning the idea of sleep altogether when I heard a tremendous crashing and tearing sound, loud enough to be audible above the wind and coming from somewhere on the river side of the house. I could connect the sound with nothing except the notion that part of the house had collapsed.

Pulling on boots and outdoor clothes, I lit a hurricane lamp and went round to the front of the house. At first I could see nothing wrong. It was not until I battled my way onto the sand bar that I could see that half the jetty had disappeared, and the broken end was hanging down in the water, part of it being dragged by the strong current, and another part torn upwards and still wrenched at by the force of the wind. I wondered what weight could have caused the end of the jetty to disintegrate so totally and so quickly. It was then that I saw a long deep furrow cut into the sand bar; following this to the other side I saw, slued against one of the giant boulders, not fifty yards from the house, two massive slabs of ice, each of about fifteen square yards and a yard thick. The first slab had apparently hit the jetty and then been turned inshore by the current and swept up onto the sand bar. The second ice-floe had followed the same course but had somehow mounted on top of the first slab and hurtled on into the boulder, smashing it open. There was something odd about these massive pieces of pack-ice and when I drew closer I could see by the light of the lamp that sealed in their cloudy depths was all kinds of garbage; bits of rope and wood, but also plastic containers and plastic bags.

Near to the house I heard someone calling my name, and I turned to see Elena. She came to where I was standing, and because it was impossible to talk above the sound of the wind, I gestured towards the jetty and towards the ice and tried to explain to her what had made the terrible noise that must have disturbed her. As we turned to go back into the house we saw Maria standing at the balcony balustrade above us, her black hair billowing out behind her, and her black night clothes flattened against her body.

Once inside Elena wanted me to come with her to the balcony-room to tell Maria what had happened; she seemed to think that the sooner Maria was reassured that all was well, then the sooner she would go back to her bed. But when we reached the balcony-room it was empty. I put some wood on the embers in the fireplace and poured us each a brandy. We stood in one of the windows looking out into the darkness, seeing and hearing the wind whip up the frozen snow from the balcony and lash it hard against the glass. Certainly I had never known a wind of this fury to coincide with such low temperatures; it seemed a combination that was strange and unnatural. But on the other hand I knew also that storm winds were always short lived on the river.

"What does it mean, the ice?" Elena asked me.

"It means that if the wind continues to blow from the east then there will be even colder weather to come. The ice has come from the other side of the river, from the harbor of a town or a city somewhere upstream. And it has not melted away naturally but has been broken up, probably by the use of explosives."

"Is it possible that the entire river could freeze?" Elena asked.

"I do not know. I suppose that it is possible."

"And then would people, the people on the other side, come across here; simply wander across or drive across, I mean?"

"To them the river is a kind of security zone; they are taught to be wary of this side, even to fear it. I do not think that they would cross."

Elena was silent for some time, and standing beside her I was suddenly aware of the uniqueness of this situation. We had both been disturbed by the crashing ice, and had both ventured out into the howling gale to

investigate; now we stood together in the middle of the
night, a task of joint guardianship accomplished as it
were; we had ascertained that all was safe, and had
thereby enabled the others to sleep on undisturbed.

And though the tension and wariness still existed
between us as we stood looking out from the window,
nevertheless I felt an unusual sense of familiarity or
companionship that was entirely new to me.

She half turned towards me and spoke my name;
and the tone of her voice was so gentle and clear that
instantly complex layers of distrust and antagonism
were swept away and I found myself looking at a beautiful young woman with whom I shared a house, yet
about whom I knew almost nothing.

"Thomas, I have wanted to talk to you about
Christina." Her speech was hesitant and uncertain.
"There are things that must be said. But first you
must question me. Do you understand? I cannot
speak until you have asked certain questions; only
then can I tell you. And Thomas, time is running out,
you must act soon."

As she spoke I seemed to feel that I understood
what she was saying; and though there were no questions in my mind for me to ask, I sensed that they were
near to my consciousness, only fractionally beyond my
reach, and with her help I could discover them. And
then she would answer and I would understand.

But at that moment Genia came into the room and
stood between us. I saw that she took Elena's hand and
then, without looking at me and after a pause, she took
mine also.

Going back down to my room I felt pleased that we had had the beginnings of a conversation and I thought that it would be possible to continue it soon; I was pleased too that Genia seemed to have forgiven me.

I dozed for a few hours but got up early to go to look again at the damage to the jetty. The snow had not melted, nor had the ice, but the wind had calmed considerably. The day was overcast and the temperature still well below freezing.

The half of the jetty that remained seemed to be fairly firm and stable. It was a pity about the damage, especially as I had put a great deal of work into repairing it, but it was anyway never used. The boats were not used any more, and since the jetty was very narrow it was not possible to walk side by side with someone else on it, nor to pass them if they were coming the other way. Nor was there any pleasure in sitting at the end on one's own, looking down into the filthy water.

I walked on towards the cove. At some distance I could see that a great deal of garbage had been blown up onto the beach. Picking her way carefully through this detritus, looking down and studying everything was Bella. She was dragging behind her a brown sack. Every so often she stopped, picked up some object, usually it seemed something made of wood, and having inspected it closely either tossed it away or placed it in the sack.

I returned to the house for a rake and some matches and starting at the end of the cove that she had already scoured, I began to heap the rubbish up into great piles. When I came level with her I asked her if she had finished searching. She nodded, and suggested that we try to set all the bonfires alight at once. I agreed, but

warned her that they would burn very quickly and that
the heat would be intense; it was essential to keep well
clear because the pebbles would explode and send red
hot splinters in all directions.

When the fires were all alight and burning furiously,
we stood well back near to the place where the old rowing boats had been laid up years before. We watched as
the red and yellow flames licked ravenously at the oil
soaked wood and rope and at the melting gaudy plastic.
Bella put her sack into one of the boats, and sat across
the bow as she stared intently at the fires. She wore a
long, dark green robe; her head was thrown back, and
uncharacteristically she planted her feet well apart in
the sand; she seemed to try to thrust her belly forward
as if to remind me of our meeting on the previous day.

"I forgot to tell you." She shouted to me. "In the
night, Christina was calling for you."

I returned at once to the house, annoyed that Bella
had not given me the news immediately. Passing
through the kitchen, Nina repeated to me that Christina
had been calling out for me and that everybody had
been searching for me. Outside the balcony room Elena
told me that Christina was upstairs with Rebecca, and
that she was waiting for me.

When I burst through the door to Rebecca's room, it
was Maria who was sitting by her bed. Rebecca seemed
in a state of agitation, trying to move her arms and trying to speak. I demanded to know where Christina was.
Maria turned towards me slowly and told me that as far
as she knew the girl had locked herself in the schoolroom and was only prepared to open the door to me.

I raced down to the schoolroom, but the door was wide open and the room apparently empty. I searched quickly under the desks, behind cupboards and in the small anteroom that contained the stationery and books, but she was not there. I went quickly to the studio, my heart pounding in my chest, and tried the door that at first seemed locked. I called out her name, banged on the door, shouted out her name; and then I turned the handle properly and the door opened.

Christina was at the far end of the room, pressed into the corner as far as she could go, a terrified expression on her face. She wore only a thin white dress and her feet were bare. I called out to her that it was me Thomas, but she screamed back at me that I should go away, leave her alone, not touch her, never touch her.

I tried to calm her, tried to calm myself. I spoke quietly, closed the door behind me quietly. I said that of course I would not harm her. I began to ask what had happened to frighten her so. I moved towards her slowly so that she could reach out a hand and touch and know me. But she merely grew more agitated and fled from the corner, smashing hard against furniture as she ran. I realized that she was not yet accustomed to Maria's reorganization of her room; and then as she ran and suddenly tripped and fell heavily to the floor, I saw that she was tethered at the ankle by a long piece of rope.

Searching frantically in the cupboards until I found a knife, I managed to get close enough to her so that I could use it to hack through the rope. But at the same moment she found the window catch in her hand and wrenching it open, she hurled herself through in her mad panic to escape me.

From the window I saw her pick herself up from the
deep snow on the balcony below and stagger towards
the balustrade; without pausing she leapt this too in a
single bound.

When I turned back into the room Elena was standing in the door to the studio, a small handgun held at
eye level and pointed directly at me. But my concern
for Christina was so intense that it overrode every other
consideration and I hardly registered the threat. I raced
on and pushed past her and as I did so she lowered the
gun and continued to stare blindly at the open window.

My desperate concern was that Christina had hurt
herself when she leapt from the balcony and I went to
the front of the house as fast as I could.

There was no sign of her, merely the slightest trace
of blood in the snow where she had landed. Then I
thought I caught a glimpse of her in the cherry orchard;
I began to search it thoroughly, tree by tree, aware that
her slender form could so easily be hidden by one of
the tree trunks. But she was not to be found there either.

I saw a movement at some distance out in the scrub-
land and though it was difficult to be certain because of
the white of her dress against the snow, nevertheless I
was sure that it was her. I began to run after her, but after
a few minutes I stopped. I knew that I would not catch up
with her before she reached the forest, and in any event I
could run no more until I had rested and regained my
breath. I sank down against one of the trees.

There came into my mind then the image of Maria
sitting by Rebecca's bed as I had seen her a short while
before and there rose in me the most violent rage
against her. I wanted to leap like an animal at the white

flesh of her neck and to sink my teeth in there and to hold on until in her struggle to get free she broke her back; and then on and on until in terrible pain she bled to death. Only then would I release her, only when I was sure beyond a shadow of a doubt that she was truly dead. I longed to witness her destruction, the great bulk of her body, bloodless and lifeless. And even as I felt this fury, I knew that it arose from my immediate recognition of the part her vile mind had played in the tragedy that had befallen Christina.

I took the truck and drove to the cabin at the edge of the forest. There I began to search methodically until I found her footprints which as I had expected led on into the trees. With a small axe I made a notch on a tree at the point where the footprints disappeared and continued on into the forest marking the trees as I went.

Large branches weighed down with ice had broken free and crashed down and these made progress very difficult; there were giant ferns and creepers which made it almost impossible to see for any distance. And sometimes the scattered boulders were heaped up into great mounds that barred the way. I dared not venture too far for fear of becoming totally lost. All I could do was to search the fringe of the forest, keeping the scrub-land just in sight, and continue to call her name. Every so often I stopped to listen, shout her name, and listen.

But there was no response; an absolute silence except for the occasional tearing crash as another over-burdened branch fell to the forest floor.

I could not give up. I trudged many miles in one direction, returned until I found again the trees that I had marked, and then searched many miles in the other direction; and all the time I called her name. Finally I climbed to the top of one of the great pyramids of boulders and sat gazing hopelessly about me. I knew that it was already too late to find her. In her thin dress and with bare feet she was perhaps safe for as long as she could keep moving; but in that temperature, once she stopped to rest she would quickly become too cold to recover; she would shiver violently, then become still and quickly die.

The snow had not penetrated the forest canopy, but all the upper branches were heavy with ice and snow; the strange light filtering through the trees and reflected by them, was a weak, luminous green, as if I was under the sea, and it made all the vegetation seem brittle and insubstantial. Though I was frozen to the bone I was not yet ready to go back to the house.

I had been such a fool; I had walked straight into the trap that they had so carefully laid for me. Their dreams and false dreams, warnings and false warnings had all lured me gently yet precisely towards this end–the loss of Christina, the loss of the one among them whom I most cherished. They had re-organized her room, tethered her, filled her head with mad fears that I would harm her; and then they had ensured that in my concern I would blunder wildly into her room, thus precipitating the exact outcome that they wished to see.

Overwhelmed by a sense of loss and too devastated and stunned to weep, I could hardly bear to think that even then she might still be very close to me and still alive, afraid to call out, afraid of me. If I could find her in time, wrap her frail form in my coat, carry her quickly to the cabin, light a fire..... But I could not find her, and it was already much too late.

I thought of the house which had always had for me its still, calm center, the sanctity of the studio where this beautiful, creative, harmless being dwelt in her own darkness. Now she was gone, and the heart of the house was empty, cold and dead.

Impelled by the same cold, I climbed down from the pyramid of boulders and made my way slowly out of the forest. I drove back to the house cautiously, taking no risks. The place was in silence. I went straight to the studio and locked myself in.

There was the rope, one end attached to the leg of the large bookcase, the other frayed where I had hacked at it with the knife. Her bed was neatly made and folded down ready for her sleep. There was the sculpture that she had been working on, covered in a plastic sheet; this I removed and stared as if in a trance at the likeness of Elena. For a moment I thought that I might smash it to pieces, but I changed my mind and replaced the cover. I sat down near to the radiator and became warm.

I gazed about the room, half curious to look in detail at all her things, half aware in my fatigue that I would never again hear her voice in this room, or watch her in the mirror, or hear her reminding me that she would give me lessons if only I would come to her in the early evenings.

I remembered that only a few days ago I had studied her eyes closely and perhaps my intention had been that I would carry the image with me in my mind, better than any photograph. But even now the image was fading; I could not recall, though I tried my utmost, the exact shape of her eyes, nor whether her lower lashes were long or short; whether she wore a ring on her right hand, nor the precise line of her nose. At once I began searching in cupboards and drawers for other photographs of Christina, convinced that there must be some. But I found nothing but endless postcards of other women: angels, heroines, lorelei, dancers, dark and fair, naked and clothed, young and old, black and white, strong and weak...

I began to talk aloud to myself, telling the room that her hair was fair and long, her eyes blue and strong...

But I was falling asleep, exhausted by the events of the day. I got to my feet and unlocked the door to the studio.

On the landing outside, Elena was sitting in the shadows and she caught my sleeve as I passed.

"I have shot her." She said.

"Shot who?"

"Maria." She said. "She is dead."

I sat on the seat beside her, but I said nothing. After a while she got up and walked slowly away from me, and shortly I followed and went to my bed.

Six

The news of Maria's death did not surprise me; there was something inevitable, even natural about it. It seemed to follow on logically from everything else that had happened, and indeed to be the climax of those events. I felt a quiet sense of relief and release; release from the debilitating burden of the violent fantasies centered on her that racked my body and mind. No more need I be possessed by those vile images, no more taken over by an impotent rage. I was free. This was good news; I was free to live my life, to move about the house without being constantly aware of her presence, her scornful eye, her disapproval, her phony protection. In a moment a great complex of bad feeling had been swept away. It was as if she had not existed, and I could barely recall her to mind, and then only with a sense of slight distaste. I no longer had to eat that food, feel that guilt, control those feelings.

I went to Maria's room and tapped on the door; it was Frieda's voice that called me in. She was sitting at one side of the bed, and she motioned me to sit in a chair on the opposite side. Maria's vast bulk lay on the bed entirely covered by a white sheet. It was a great white mound, the summit of which was her bloated stomach. I wondered how we would be able to dispose of such a giant corpse.

For Frieda's sake I tried to keep calm and quiet and suitably solemn as I sat by the bed, but she saw that I was exhausted and she told me to sleep; she told me to lean forward onto the bed and to go to sleep for a while. She would wake me soon. I rested my head on my hands on the edge of the bed and immediately fell into a deep sleep.

I awoke gradually to a realization of where I was and what had happened. My arms had slipped close to the white sheet and I withdrew them quickly. Frieda still sat by the bed, watching me, watching the body. When I was fully awake and had sat back in my chair, she got up and began to pull back the sheet. I had expected her merely to uncover Maria's head, but she removed it completely, and I was amazed to see that the body was totally naked.

Every inch of her flesh was almost perfectly white, except her nipples and lips which were a pale gray-pink. Her long hair spread out on the pillow was now also white, and I could only assume that when she had been washed the black dye had been rinsed away. Her arms lay at her sides, her legs slightly apart; her eyes were closed. The skin was not wrinkled or puckered but quite taut, shining and tight over all her body and face. But what really surprised me as I gazed at her was what I felt and did not feel.

There was no feeling of repugnance; she seemed instead strangely attractive like some favorite household god that had at last been unearthed, strong and splendid in her nakedness. She should always have gone naked, I thought; it was her clothes that spoilt her and made her so hateful.

I did not feel sorrow exactly, but something akin to that emotion; as if she had been sacrificed. It had been a tragedy, inevitable and therefore sad; but it was a sadness that gave me strength. I reached out my hand to touch her, but thought for a moment that I might be doing wrong and looked to Frieda for permission. She said almost in a whisper, Touch, yes, touch her.

I grasped Maria's arm just above the wrist; the flesh was firm and cold. Nevertheless though the arm was beginning to broaden out towards the elbow, the feel or texture was like a young woman's arm, a girl's arm, smooth and delicate, weak and yet strong; and giving rise to contrary emotions, like the beginning of desire.

I held her hand and pulled it across the bedcovers towards me; and as I did so the wound was revealed. It was in her side at the level of her waist. A dark hole, its center bordered by red and yellow skin, only slightly jagged and no longer bleeding. And though it seemed harmless enough, it was a blemish on her skin, a strange lesion that would now never heal.

"Did she die quickly?" I asked.

"Instantly. In my arms. She said nothing." Frieda's tone of voice was passive, quite free of her customary reserve and tension.

"Thomas, I want you to think about her and remember her."

For some time as I sat and held onto Maria's hand, only the most mundane thoughts entered my mind. I considered her life from the beginning, but since I knew so few details about her, it became the life of any woman. There were words and images: child, female child, clothes, hair, gentleness, discovery, strength, puberty, blood, boys, love, marriage, childbirth, and so on. But then gradually I began to recall details of specific events in and around the house during the last few years.

But though there must have been hundreds, thousands of occasions and meetings and meal-times when there had been no conflict, no overt antagonism or anger, I could remember nothing that was not negative and disturbing. Memory upon memory brought back instantly the anger of the occasion again, exactly as it had been felt then; and sometimes worse, sometimes it was recalled with an increased sense of violence and despair. And with these feelings also a nagging, damning sense of regret, or shame; shame that I had been so often embroiled in situations that were so stupid and childish, so commonplace and meaningless.

And now there was in my mind all that anger and hate piled high upon itself, coiled round itself exactly as if a snake writhed and twisted within my gut as it tried to get free. This fury seemed to spread like a disease throughout my body; it became also an anger at my loneliness, anger directed against the other women, anger at the pollution, anger that Rebecca would not get up from her bed, anger that Frieda would say nothing, anger that Bella's children died, anger with all the world; anger with myself because I was so angry, and maddened further that I seemed incapable of escaping this torment, this nightmare of rage.

I saw the middle finger of my left hand, and it rested near to the wound in Maria's body. I spoke aloud, saying to myself.

"All this, all this anger, this foul memory, this sickness, surely it cannot be suffered. Surely it should be ignored, buried, forgotten, wiped from memory, eliminated cleanly and clearly just as a disease is eradicated from the face of the earth. Surely it cannot be important, I cannot believe that it can be important..."

And in my anxiety to throw off physically this weight that oppressed me, I thrust out my arms before me and the finger of my left hand entered the wound in her side, deep into the wound itself. No sooner had I sensed the warmth at the tip of my finger than a pain, a great agony seized my gut. I withdrew my finger at once and slumped back in the chair, but the seizure did not cease. Then I saw that something was oozing from the wound, not blood but a thick, yellowy-white fluid; it poured forth in a continuous stream, down over her side, gradually filling the indentation that her body made in the bed.

The terrible pain in my stomach continued unabated and the tallow continued to flow from her; and as it built up in the hollow of the bed around her, so it set like a kind of wax. There was a strange movement in her hand that I held, a rhythmic pulse, and I saw that the fat fingers became slender, the fat arms thin, and the belly gently subsided as the fluid continued to be shed. There was no odor, no sound. The river of tallow flowed silently from her, and her body shrank, smaller and thinner until she was a frail old woman, pure skinned, not over-wrinkled, held or framed in the oval pool that was setting firm about her. And as the suffering in my belly eased, so the flow of liquid dried up and the wound disappeared.

On her body there were a few marks of age, but no other blemish was to be seen. The tallow had lifted her in the bed somewhat and in the process her body had curled and turned on its side towards me; her arms were raised and the palms of her small hands came together. The color of her skin, the neatness of her body, the lightness of her long hair, the softness and stillness of her form, all these things reminded me for a moment of Christina.

Frieda got up and went to a cupboard in the room and returned with a small cardboard box. From this she took a number of silver rings and bracelets which she passed to me. I put them onto Maria's fingers and around her wrists. Whether Frieda intended it or not, this action made me understand clearly that this woman had once been young; young and slender, full of vigor and love of life.

Frieda pulled up the sheet and tucked it in around Maria's chin so that only her face was uncovered.

"Is this the woman you loathed?" she asked quietly.

"No, no." I shook my head. "She is transformed."

"Yet for so long you chose to hate her?"

"I did not choose. I could do nothing else. She presented such a vile face to me. She never had a kind word for me, nor respected me, nor loved me..."

"And you craved the love and respect, and you could not be civilized without the kind word? You could not see beyond appearance, beyond the mask? You understand now, Thomas, that all your hate was directed at this stuff, this tallow, which now that it has been drained, reveals another woman. Why could you not have tried to approach her during all this time; to listen to her feelings and thoughts?"

"Frieda, I tried, again and again I tried. She was terrified that I would take Christina away from her, terrified of the indignity of that event. She would not listen to me."

"But, Thomas, you wanted to take Christina away. This has always been true, and Maria knew that it was true."

The mention of Christina's name filled me with a sense of hopelessness, of weakness, and of mild aimless anger. But this anger was directed not against Frieda, who had given me good warning, not even against Maria, but simply against myself. Why had I delayed? How deep was my regret that I had not, years before, taken Christina away from the house.

"I should have taken her away." I said. "Saved her..."

"Saved her? Saved her from this frail old woman?" Frieda gestured towards the body of Maria lying curled between us. "Where would you have taken her?"

"To the other side, perhaps," I replied.

"Thomas you are a stubborn man becoming a stubborn old man; why so rigid and unyielding? What is there to gain? You merely continue to live your half life with your half suffering. Your fantasy world; your destructive, wasteful fantasy. If you had taken Christina

you would not have known what to say to her, what to
ask, what to hear and what to ignore; you do not know
her, you have not spoken to her, therefore how can you
love her?"

"Is it such a mystery?"

"If you ask such a question then I fear that you are
less prepared for life than I had thought. Still you do not
see us as we are, nor hear us, nor take us seriously. We
still do not really exist for you; we are mere shadows.
And that, Thomas, is a great sadness to me. I am an old
woman, and I cannot be patient for ever."

She was silent for some time. I considered the impos-
sibility of expressing my feelings; the sense of complex-
ity, and perplexity, and quiet madness that I felt when
confronted with these vague, emotional, unreasonable
accusations. It was hopeless, everything was hopeless; I
had always imagined that one day I would talk openly
and deeply with Frieda; that I would explain myself, my
struggle and confusion, and that she would understand,
comment and sympathize. But face to face now, what
was I hearing; an ambiguous, formless quarrel with
every tenet by which I lived.

"I know, Thomas," she continued, "that you still
intend to leave us, to abandon us. To run away, to chase
phantoms and chimeras, to turn your back on the real
world around you; to ignore us, to waste us; and in so
doing to condemn yourself to your sterile cell for all time.

"But have we not shouted out to you loud enough
and clearly enough and often enough. Have we not
shown you the richness of reality, and will you not now
live. Will you not learn tact, tenderness, insight; will you
not learn of ambiguity, of mystery and of unconditional

love. Of deep feelings, Thomas, that would be so strong
within you that you could no longer ignore them?

"But I fear that you will fail. I fear that you will
become less than you are; vulnerable and terrified of
attack, you will shrink inside your shell and hardly daring to show your face, spit out mad doctrines at all who
come near. An ordinary man, but vicious, letting the
world die around him."

But the viciousness seemed hers. I could not understand why Frieda should have chosen that time to make
such a pointless and negative analysis of my state of
mind. It seemed unworthy of her, and made it difficult
for me to feel I could rely on her calm intelligence.

But she was right in one respect at least, that as she
talked I was considering again the possibility or
inevitability of leaving the house; I had begun to assess
the pros and cons, to weigh them in the balance and to
wonder what effect my absence would have on them all.
Looking at Frieda I felt at that moment a strong desire to
prove to her beyond any shadow of a doubt that I could
easily and without effort stand on my own feet, live my
own life, be free of them. She had issued a challenge to
me and I was almost ready to decide to take it up.

As I was leaving Maria's room Frieda asked me to
place a low table in the aisle of the chapel and also to
send Nina to her, and these things I did. I saw that it
was almost dawn.

I wandered about the house, listening at doors,
standing still on the landings and in the halls, waiting, as
it were, for a feeling of certainty; certainty that I knew

what I was doing, that I was in control; or certainty that any action I took would indeed be inevitable, the only course open to me, a course forced upon me by circumstances beyond my control.

I stared from the balcony room out across the river trying to see if by concentration I could distinguish between the land on the far side, the dense trees and small hills, and the gray-brown expanse of the early morning sky. For a moment in the far distance the sun shone through a fissure in the clouds and I was able to see a familiar landmark on the other side of the river—a small bare hill, a mere grassy knoll perhaps, which projected above the surrounding woods. On this knoll there was a single tree and since its form never seemed to change, I had long ago concluded that it was a dead tree. For a fleeting moment I could see all this, and then the sun disappeared and it was gone. I could see only the drab sky bearing down on the great dull mass of the swiftly flowing river, the river that was impossible to cross, of uncertain currents, depths and shallows, dangerous and poisonous in every yard of its width.

When Nina came to find me we went together to Maria's room. She told me that she had carried the body to the chapel. We stood at each side of the bed, contemplating the elliptical pool of hardened tallow, in the center of which was a perfect impression of Maria's form. We decided that it must be broken into more manageable pieces and taken to the cove, there to be burnt.

At the cove we first raked together the remains of the flotsam and jetsam that had not already been burnt and heaped this up into a kind of pyre. We made an attempt to arrange the tallow on the top of this in something like its original form. We worked together in silence and even when Genia arrived, curious to know what we were doing, no one spoke. When the pyre was lit the wax began to melt and flow over the pebbles that surrounded it, and then onwards towards the water, some of it floating on the surface where it hardened again. Suddenly the tallow at the center of the fire burst into flame that immediately also ignited the area all around the pyre; then, as if it had suddenly found a way of escape, the flame roared its way down the beach and ignited even the wax that floated on the surface of the water. It was an incredible sight, the vigor and fury of the flames, the colors of red and yellow and green and blue; and the angry black smoke curling and twisting up into the cold air.

It was more than an hour before everything was burned; there remained only a thin layer of fine white ash on the pebbles that was soon lifted by the wind and dispersed.

There followed a form of funeral service in the chapel. Maria's body now clothed in a plain white dress that cannot have been her own, was lying on a simple mattress on the small table that I had placed there. Frieda sat in one of the chairs near to the altar, gazing directly ahead of her. Genia, Elena, and Nina were seated on the other chairs. Rebecca had not been brought to the chapel. Bella knelt at the altar, silent for a moment, clutching in her upraised hands some object that had belonged to Maria. It seemed to be the small, silver-backed mirror and frequently it reflected the flame from the candles and sent shafts of light darting about the ceiling of the chapel.

Bella began to wail, a low monotonous noise, and then to sway violently backwards and forwards. I saw Frieda rise quickly to calm or restrain her, and at the same moment I rose quietly from my seat and left the room.

Since it was impossible to dig a grave in the frozen ground, Genia had suggested that we place Maria in one of the old boats that were beached near the cove and simply let her float down the river. I decided that I had best go to inspect the boats closely; they had not been in the water for so many years and I did not know if any of them would still float.

All three boats seemed in remarkably good order, and I chose the smallest, an old fashioned, very solid and well-made boat with an attractive and ornamental sweep upwards at both the bow and the stern. Much of the colored paint-work had long since peeled off, but the red stripe that encircled it was still clearly visible, as were the remnants of the green and yellow decoration of leaves and flowers at the bow.

Having cleared the boat of debris and snow, I attached a short rope. I was having difficulty dragging it towards the water when Elena arrived and began to help me; no doubt she too had been driven away from the funeral service in the chapel. When we had launched the boat she caught hold of my arm.

"Thomas, if I had known..." Her voice was tense and harsh, though she seemed to be appealing for my understanding.

"Yes, yes," I said. "I must get the boat over to the jetty."

"But Thomas, Christina..."

But I could not bear to think about Christina at that moment, nor talk to Elena about her, and I walked away towing the boat behind me.

I maneuvered it all the way around the bay and along the bank until I reached the jetty, being careful not to step in the water or be splashed by it. I tied the boat up and waited there for the end of the funeral service.

We carried out the mattress with the body on it and placed it across the rowing seats in the boat. Genia was afraid that the boat might rock violently in the rapid flow of the river and the body be thrown out so she returned to the house and collected a number of bright silk scarves and with these I tied the body firmly in place. Some around her ankles, some her wrists, and another tightly across her shoulders. Genia arranged the dress as best she could in the cold wind, and lamented the fact that we had no flowers. Maria's face was pale and at peace, and the silver rings and bracelets and the bright colors of the scarves made her seem elegant and graceful.

I towed the boat out to the end of what remained of the jetty, pulled the rudder over to make sure that the boat went as far out as possible into the mid-stream and pushed it off as hard as I could. Her white dress lifted slightly and the ends of the colored scarves flapped in the wind. The boat continued for fifty yards across the flow and then turned suddenly downstream and moved away from us very quickly.

The others returned into the house soon afterwards; I watched them go, a small sad group, hurrying away into the warmth. I waited on the jetty until the boat was a mere speck in the distance. It seemed to me that

Maria had escaped, got away from it all, and I envied her. Genia had hoped that she would be carried far out to sea, but I knew that it would be unlikely at this time of year that the boat would pass freely through the myriad channels of the delta; no doubt the boat with its strange cargo would be stranded somewhere within the delta itself and would only be lifted free to continue its journey to the sea when the flood waters came in the spring.

As I walked back I realized that the house would be quite changed without Maria; calmer, less dangerous, less fraught, and full of new possibilities. Yet these good things could not even begin to alleviate the pain at the loss of Christina; without her the house was without meaning.

I went first to my room, gathering things together, and then to the kitchen, taking a few provisions and a few bottles of wine. I left the house quietly, spent some time digging the truck out of the snow, and drove in the direction of the cabin. Once there, I told myself, I could concentrate my energies on the search for Christina's body; and at the same time my proximity to the forest would enhance the glimmer of hope that I had that she was somehow still alive.

I would live in the cabin until my search was complete, one way or another. I would never return. They would see that I did not need them, and that I had no real affinity with them; that they were outside me, outside my world, and that the scant feelings that I had for them would disappear into thin air as soon as I was free of the house.

Seven

The drive was slow and difficult. On arrival I worked hard before it grew dark to prepare the cabin for my first night. I cleared the snow that had in places drifted almost to the windows. I brought in wood and stacked it to dry on each side of the stove and I brought in buckets of snow so that it would begin to melt. I draped the blankets from the bed all around the room to air so that my bedding would not be damp. And I tidied and swept out the entire cabin, getting rid of all that was not needed. I put my few books on the shelf above the bed, set out my paper and pen on one end of the table, and covered the other, on which I would eat, with a small cloth. I stacked the wine close to the door, and hung up on a peg my spare clothes; made a decision as to which of the enamel bowls would be for washing dishes and so on, and which for ablutions. I stuffed newspapers in some of the holes around the windows, and nailed up bits of material as curtains; and when it grew dark I put the bar across the door. I lit the oil lamp and a candle and piling wood on the stove until it roared, I threw open the small door at the front and pulled a chair up close. I leant forward and felt the heat on my face; and soon I was warm and beginning to feel the exhaustion against which I had been fighting for so long.

It was wonderful to be alone in the cabin. I opened a bottle of good red wine and set it and a glass on a small table beside me. I felt too tired to drink, but nevertheless I felt that I should salute my decision, congratulate myself and confirm myself in my resolution, though I had no doubt that I had done the right thing. I was tired and I could not remember the last time that I had slept properly, yet through this fatigue I could sense my excitement; I was at last free. Tomorrow I would begin to restore and strengthen myself in body and mind, and begin to build a new life. There would be no looking back, no thought about them, not a shred of curiosity about their fate; only a serious and methodical search for Christina who would now be found...

I sat there long into the night, occasionally aware of the wind beating against the window, occasionally putting more wood on the fire; and I drank the bottle of wine. In my mind, unbidden, an endless, almost ceremonial skirmish took place; first a memory, a bad memory, a distasteful image, an image of defeat or ignominy occupied an arena like an angry, wounded lion, prowling and roaring, knowing that it was trapped; then the adversary, myself, armed and mounted on a black horse. There followed precise movements; not a word was spoken, no sign of fear, as the animal was destroyed with a single, triumphant thrust of the sword.

I would watch to the end; the horses entering the arena, the dead lion attached by chains and dragged away across the dry sand... and a sip or two of wine to calm my nerves and to confirm my sense of satisfaction and justice.

But there was no peace, the success would be short-lived; within a few moments I was challenged again; there appeared a seemingly endless succession of maimed, ferocious animals seeking vengeance.

On the morning of my first day I awoke much later than I had intended; I did not sleep well and I was extremely cold, but as soon as I had re-lit the fire and made some coffee I began to feel better. I heated water and shaved myself. I reorganized the bed to make it more comfortable, wondering whether I should drag it from the bedroom nearer to the fire, but deciding against this. I brought in more wood, telling myself that I must try to use less than I had on the previous evening.

Unsure of what to do next, I stood staring from the window, slipping away into a dream, when suddenly I felt Genia's arms about me and I turned quickly to face her; but of course there was no one.

Angry with myself, I looked away from the window, away from the house, and cursed aloud that I was so susceptible to these memories, so impressionable that I had been convinced for a moment that she stood behind me and had encircled me with her arms. I was beginning to understand the cunning ways in which they would try to communicate with me, how they would try to catch my attention when I was least prepared, possessing my mind by shrewd and subtle calculations, bringing me to my knees with a single well-aimed blow. I must be on my guard, at all times alert and ready to fend off surprise attacks. I must keep occupied, never allow my mind to become empty or still.

I went out into the snow and found the place that I had marked where I had found Christina's footprints. I ventured into the forest a short distance. I had brought with me a compass in order to convince myself that it would indeed be a useless instrument because of the magnetic rocks. It was as I had been told; the compass needle remained quite steady for a short distance and then suddenly shuddered violently and pointed in a completely different direction. Following this line for a short distance, I soon came across a place where the boulders were heaped up into a giant mound forming a magnetic source easily able to influence the compass.

I returned to the cabin and ate and satisfied my hunger. I then set about formulating a plan, some system whereby I could search for Christina while eliminating the risk of being lost in the forest. I believed that I had devised the best way, and I gathered together as much rope as I could find from the logging site, the cabin itself and the truck. I spent the evening unravelling this rope into its three or four or sometimes five strands and then winding these cords in fifty yard lengths onto pieces of wood. I calculated that I had over one thousand yards of cord in all, and I was convinced that this was enough for the search.

That evening I was disciplined; I slowly ate a light meal and went to bed feeling strong and determined.

I awoke early on the second day; I had slept well, been warm and comfortable, and no dreams had spoiled my rest. Immediately I went outside, even before I was properly dressed. The temperature was still well below freezing and during the night it had snowed again, sufficient to obscure all my tracks and movements around the cabin made on the previous day. I began to do physical exercises, at first to keep warm, but then for the pleasure of it. I began to run in a wide circle about the cabin, leaping logs, running the length of one of the fallen trees, and half-shouting, half-singing as I did so. I felt energetic and healthy. It was good to be alive, and I was pleased to be alone in this wild and rugged place.

When I went back inside to finish dressing and to light the stove to make coffee, I realized that this was what I had been waiting for, this release, this sense of freedom and simple joy, unencumbered by the deviousness and intricacy and anxiety that existed in the house; that tiresome and endless and pointless round of feeling and counter-feelings that nagged away at me day after day and sapped my strength. I felt sure that I had discovered the world of reality, the point from which everything new must emerge; man alone in nature, dependent solely on his own mind and body, his own skill and dexterity and speed. The idea was exhilarating, even beautiful, and I knew that I would increase my strength and my vitality on certain conditions; that I concentrated my mind, denying all dreams, stifling them at birth; that I rigorously controlled my desires; and that I guard against a recurrence of the negative influence of the women. I needed to arm myself against sentimentality, weakness, and all doubt.

When I had sawed and chopped enough wood for at least two or three days, I piled the rope cords onto the truck and drove the short distance along the edge of the forest to the point where I had marked the trees. I packed all my spindles of cord in a sack and tied a rope to this, and though it was very heavy I was just able to carry it on my back. When I was at the last of my marked trees within the forest I attached the cord to a tree, and as I moved further into the forest so I gradually unwound it.

My progress was very slow; in order to save cord I wanted to keep to as straight a course as possible and this meant that frequently I had to climb over piles of boulders and at times hack my way through areas of dense creeper. While letting out the cord, I was at the same time searching for Christina. Every few minutes I would put down the rope and the sack from my back and search for her nearby under the enormous ferns, behind trees, and in the crevices formed between the boulders. It was perhaps an almost hopeless task, yet I believed that my thoroughness must be rewarded. What I had underestimated was the amount of time that the search would require.

When I had reached the end of the cord I retraced my steps, winding up the cord as I went and carefully putting each fifty yard length back in the sack; and even then as I returned I searched for a sign of Christina's presence.

Once I was back in the scrub-land it was my intention to move along the forest edge for about a hundred yards and then began to repeat the whole procedure. But though my cord was about one thousand yards in length, I journeyed into the forest for only about seven hundred yards perhaps because it was impossible due to the trees, boulders, ferns, and creepers to keep to anything other than a zig-zag course; nevertheless I felt sure that she was unlikely to have been able to penetrate the forest even to that depth. She must have been exhausted, almost frozen before she even reached the forest.

As I was on the return and winding up the cord, I thought I saw her, her white dress and white skin near to a boulder; but when I came near to the spot I saw that it was a branch of a tree from the canopy and some snow that had fallen with it. But strangely it gave me hope, and I continued with greater determination.

My next attempt was on the other side of the first, thus ensuring that I covered most thoroughly the territory nearest to where I had first sighted her footprints. It proved to be a particularly difficult place with more fallen branches and underbrush than usual. I was beginning to find that the peculiar light affected my eyes, making it difficult to focus. Perhaps I had grown too accustomed to the snow; perhaps it was something to do with the oil lamp in the cabin. I began to stumble and quite often to fall so that my ankles and arms were becoming scraped and bruised.

Shortly after I turned to begin my retreat I found that the cord had been severed; the end was frayed and wet and had obviously been gnawed through by some animal, but I found the other end without difficulty and tied a knot. Later, however, the same thing occurred again, but this time when I managed at last to find the other end it was only a few yards in length. It turned out that about thirty yards of cord had been attacked and bitten into numerous smaller lengths so that it was only with great difficulty and with mounting panic that I was able to find the place where the cord continued undamaged and so find my way as quickly as possible back to the scrub-land. It was a clear warning of the risk that I was taking; it disturbed me that I did not even see or hear the animals that threatened me in this way.

Before my fourth attempt I sat down just within the forest itself and lit a small fire in a protected place between two of the boulders. I got out from my sack a half-filled bottle of wine and I huddled against one of the stones and settled to consider my progress so far.

It seemed strange that I had not found her. I wondered whether I should go over the same ground for a second time. I considered too what I would do when I found her; to bury her, or burn her. I would burn her. But first I would gather her frozen body in my arms and embrace and kiss her; and while kissing her I might notice her blind eyes moving behind the closed lids...

The wind was getting up and beginning to penetrate my clothing, so I decided to abandon the search for that day and to continue early on the following morning when I would decide probably to go over the same ground again. It had been a good day, though I was disappointed not to have found her. Nevertheless it had been a purposeful and thorough search and I was pleased to have proved that it was possible to make the effort and to endure. I was tired as I drove back to the cabin, tired and cold, but I was not dispirited.

As I opened the cabin door I disturbed a rat that had been eating the biscuits that I had left on the table. I would have to look for some traps. I could not bear the idea of this kind of infestation, apart from the fact that I had few rations in any case.

As I was thinking about this and looking from the window in the direction of the house, I saw a figure approaching, someone stumbling along through the snow carrying something heavy. As the person drew closer I thought that I recognized Nina, the type of coat and scarf she wore, and perhaps also her way of walking. I watched her progress towards me with bated breath, hardly knowing what I felt, whether I would fling open the window and scream at her to go away, or whether I would go to the door, ask her what she wanted, invite her in if only for a few moments.

At about two hundred yards from the cabin she stopped and put down whatever it was that she was carrying. She stared in my direction for sometime, and then turned slowly and began to trudge back to the house. When I could no longer see her, I went out to see what she had left in the snow; it was a large black pan with handle and lid that contained soup and on top of this was a hunk of bread. Between the two there was a folded slip of paper on which there were these two words written in pencil: Come back.

In the cabin I put the soup to heat on the stove and sat close to it and re-read those two words many times before screwing up the piece of paper and throwing it into the flames. If Nina thought that the soup might entice me back she was wrong; I rationed myself carefully and excellent though it was, I managed to make it last a long time. The small piece of bread from the end of the loaf surprised me. I felt sure that she would have brought me an entire loaf; perhaps they were running out of flour.

Going to the window I pulled back the makeshift curtain. I could just make out the lights of the house, and yes, also smoke coming from at least one chimney. So they were warm and had light, and obviously had plenty of beans and vegetables to make soup.

I did not have a good evening. For some reason I could not get warm. Sitting as close as I could to the stove, I kept thinking of Nina, her humor, her smile and the warmth of her body. I became so angry at my inablity to rid my mind of her image that I grabbed a piece of burning wood from the fire and clenched it in the palm of my hand for a few seconds; the pain was excruciating, the act pointless. I looked at the wound for some time and then bandaged it as best I could. I allowed Genia's arms to encircle me, and Nina to sit naked at my feet, the glow from the fire reflected by her breasts. My anger was dissipated and became a vague melancholy; and beyond this there was a common lone-liness that I attributed to the fact that I was not yet accustomed to my solitary life.

I drank freely of the good wine and mused upon the peculiar strength of the sense of Genia's presence in the room. Almost experimentally I considered how good it might be to have the company of another man, to talk and discuss, to plan the following day, to share out the duties and responsibilities, and to confirm each other in our sense of independence. But within a few moments I was again thinking of Nina and I could not raise the energy to prevent it. When she had been sitting with me for only a few minutes by the fire, I heard Elena enter the cabin. She stood behind me and placed her hands on my shoulders and I dare not move for fear of frightening her away; without turning to look at her, I passed her my glass of wine. Sensing her take it, I let go of the glass, and it smashed into pieces on the floor around me.

How odd it seemed to me that at the end of that poor, feeble evening it was Elena whom I could not keep out of my thoughts. I went to bed calmly. I dreamt that she showed me, one by one, all the beautiful books that were kept in the studio, books of paintings, of sculpture and of exotic places; images of ancient ruined cities and of dry dusty roads winding among olive trees where one could wander, dreaming, from dawn until the end of day.

On the third day I awoke feeling drugged and ill, aches in my limbs and a severe headache. My sleep had been disturbed by the presence of the rat that had been foraging all night in the living area of the cabin. It had clambered noisily over saucepans and other stuff and though I tried to scare it away it took hardly any notice. The palm of my hand ached from the self-inflicted burn. My only consolation was that I could reasonably assume that my illness had already begun on the previous evening and that this accounted for my mood, the melancholy, and the defeat.

I pulled myself from the bed, drank large quantities of coffee, and set off in the truck to continue my search. I had decided that the previous day's searching had indeed not been thorough enough and that I must go over it again, this time more precisely, more methodically and with greater attention to detail.

It was, however, depressing to find that though I was now getting to know the area well, it took me longer to complete each section than on the previous day; tedious too that the cord was more often severed by animals and more branches fell to impede my path. By mid-afternoon I was too exhausted to go on, and too dejected to think that an hour's rest would in any way revitalize me. I returned to the cabin and climbed straight away into the bed.

I slept fitfully. I dreamed that I was making love, but I was a woman and I lay on my back, pleased and excited to be penetrated. When the love making ceased the man lifted himself off me and moved away somewhere, out of sight, beyond thought. And it was then that I woke in the dream and found to my horror that I could not change back into the man that I was; that mentally I was trapped. I pushed my hand down across my belly and I encountered hair and then quickly moved onto my thighs which were spread and onto my knees which were raised. I was a woman. I had been lured into an alien state of mind, a state of body; a kind of irreverent, foolish experiment had gone tragically wrong and now I was punished and ashamed, deeply ashamed of my indecent crime.

I lay in the bed shaking with cold, my mind haunted by memories of the women: their faces, bodies, voices, smiles, hands and eyes appearing and disappearing before me. I got up, pulled a blanket about me and placed the chair close in front of the fire. I decided that if after all this time I could not forget them, then I would for a last time face each one in turn in what I saw as an open court. I would recall them individually to mind as honestly as I could, give them a fair hearing, offer my reasons for believing them unworthy of my attention, and then pronounce judgment. And thus, I felt sure, I would finally condemn them in my eyes, and rid them from my world.

But before I could begin I heard the rat moving behind some furniture in the corner of the room. Having already found a trap I placed a piece of bait inside it and set it up on the table behind me. I had no confidence that the rat would actually enter the trap nor that my bait was in the least bit attractive to it, but nevertheless my awareness that the trap was there was useful to me and helped me to concentrate. I returned to my place before the fire and again pulled the blanket tightly around me.

Quietly I spoke Genia's name aloud, and without the least hesitation she appeared in the dock before me. Her radiant vitality and energy, her actual innocence, all this was immediately obvious to me before I began to speak; but surely it was impossible to love simultaneously both the child and the woman. I looked at her for a long time and I could find nothing to say. I wanted only to take her hand; and she reached out her hand to me. I felt only a sense of wonder, a deep gratitude that this lovely child existed.

And with Nina too, a sense of gratitude, and a dozen questions that I wanted to ask her, and a hundred things to tell her...

When Frieda appeared she at once beckoned me into her room and offered me the good brown nectar;

she began in an unknown language to tell me the secret
of comradeship between a man and an old woman so
that when the man was also old he would know the
secret of life itself...

Bella would allow me to say nothing. In a loud voice
she snapped out the word "patience." I waited for her to
continue but she said nothing. And when I began to
speak at last, she said the word again sharply and raised
her finger to silence me. I saw or knew that the drugs that
I had given her were now finished. And I knew that the
road to the town was still impassable. Soon she would
need help, soon the pain would begin to rise in her...

Rebecca reminded me immediately of the kiss
denied, and the hair that grew on her belly and onto her
thighs; was she warm enough, I wondered, had I left sufficient logs stacked at the back of the house. I knew that
I had not. There would be no hot water for her bath, and
therefore Nina would not be able to shave her...

When I thought of Elena I experienced an exaggerated sense of something like pride that I had carried her
from the balcony to Maria's bed, and later helped her
along the landing and up the stairs back to her own
room, back to Genia. But why was I so frightened of this
woman; was it possible that my fear seemed offensive to
her; could I not speak to her freely, unconditionally, as
one human being to another, as people who dwelt in the
same house? I was surprised that this had seemed for so
long impossible, amazed that my feelings for Elena were
undergoing such a remarkable transformation...

I had been sitting absolutely still for perhaps two
hours and my body was racked with aches and pains.
As I turned stiffly in the chair I heard the rat-trap slam

shut on the table behind me. In the cage, nosing at the wire frame, was a beautiful creature, long and sleek, with a fine pale brown coat and brilliant white underbelly. I picked up the trap and went outside into the night. For the first time for many days the sky was clear; there was an almost full moon and a million stars. I pulled open the sprung door of the trap and tipped it upside down, but the animal was too terrified to realize that it could escape. Finally I had to shake it out of the trap onto the snow where it eyed me for a brief moment before darting away in great leaps and bounds. I walked in a wide circle around the cabin, feeling the snow crisp and hard under my feet, watching the moon and stars whirling above me.

I went back inside, barred the door, and returned to my seat before the fire; and I began to weep.

I wept because of the mysterious beauty of the moon and the stars; I wept because I had tried to desecrate the memory of the women, and I wept because I had failed so hopelessly. I wept because I was afraid, afraid of my solitude in the cabin, that it might last forever, afraid that the pain in my hand might not cease, that it might become infected, afraid of all disease, afraid of death.

I wept for Christina who was lost, and for Maria in the open boat somewhere, cold and abandoned. I wept because I was exhausted and because I feared that I had drawn some catastrophe upon myself, and because my life was meaningless.

I wept for a world gone mad, and my part in that madness, my cruelty to the women in the house; I denied that they could be part of my life, part of me, and so they had rightly cursed me.

But after a long time, when I could cry no more, I saw clearly the cause of my suffering; I had locked up my spirit, my soul, somewhere deep within myself, hoping that eventually it would wither and die. I had failed. A half-starved being, a skeleton, survivor of a terrible war, stood before me and bellowed and begged for a chance to live.

Eventually I closed the fire and went to bed. Though the night was extremely cold, and the rat came back as I expected, I slept well. I got up and shaved myself carefully and brushed off my clothes. I lit a fire sufficient only to boil water for my coffee. I gathered together my few possessions and put them in the sack.

Having cleared the frozen snow away from the wheels of the truck, I backed it to the logging site; there I spent two hours sawing and chopping logs and loading the truck. When it would carry not a single log more, I drove to the house.

Eight

Near to the house the smell of the river was strong; I stacked most of the logs against the wall at the back of the house and the remainder I carried into the kitchen. Both the boiler and the kitchen stove were out. In my room, where I dumped my sack, I saw that ice had formed on the inside of the window and long icicles hung from beneath the balcony. The house was cold and in silence, as if it had been deserted; I began to ask myself if my return was too late.

As I entered the balcony room they turned as one towards me. Except for Bella, they were grouped closely about the fireplace; on the hearth a small, mean fire burned. Frieda sat with Genia at her feet, and Elena was standing close behind, her hands resting on the back of the chair. Nina was sitting on the hearthstone and seemed to be trying to coax some life into the miserable embers. Rebecca sat on an upright chair in the middle of the group and her body was swathed in blankets. Her sad, gray face set against the red of her hair sent a shudder of guilt and doubt through me. Was I right to have returned; and was I strong enough to face them?

Bella, who sat at the far end of the long table, did not look up as I entered the room. She was staring fixedly at her hands that were stretched out on the table before her. And though I could see that she wore a skirt that reached to the ground, apart from this she was wearing only a thin white vest that left her arms and shoulders uncovered.

For a moment I stood staring at the women, and they at me. I said that I would light the boiler and also the stove, and I left the room.

When I had done this and made sure that the heating system was working properly, I sat at the kitchen table. It was strange to be sitting there quietly in these changed circumstances; saddened by the loss of Christina and my failure to find her, but no longer angry, no longer wishing to console myself with the promise that one day I would leave—that old and cherished idea, simply to pack my few things and leave.

I drank some wine slowly, savoring each sip with a growing sense of deep pleasure. I did not so much think that I had returned home, as recognize that from nowhere else could I begin to search for a new life other than in this house and with these women.

When Nina came into the kitchen she brought a glass and sat opposite me at the table. I filled her glass and we raised them to each other and drank.

"I almost came to you," she said. Her tone of voice suggested that she regretted that she had not. "But I thought that you might be violent."

"So I gave that impression?" I replied. I recalled her cautious approach to the cabin, leaving the soup and bread at a distance because she was afraid that I might attack her. She was right to be wary, of course; I was capable of thinking anything, and capable too of acting spontaneously, both for good and for bad. I was slow to learn even the most obvious lessons.

I looked at her across the table and I desired her strongly; but I saw that everything had changed between us and that the old familiarity had gone.

She noticed the burn on my hand and she fetched the basket of bandages and ointments that she kept in the kitchen and sat down next to me. As she tended to the burn I watched her intently, sensing in her a degree of independence or self-sufficiency that I had been unaware of before. She was changed; though she seemed physically younger, nevertheless it was as if the young woman I had known had developed all kinds of powers and strengths that I would normally have associated with someone of greater age. I put out my hand and touched the side of her face and ran my hand over her hair to her neck, stroking her. I was trying to ask what had happened; I was trying to say that it was safe to approach me, and that my love for her was like a cool, clear pool of underground water at which she could drink whenever she wished. I wanted her to know that her presence enabled me to experience a sense of time without end, an eternity, and that I was filled with quiet excitement because my patience was suddenly infinite.

We sat in the kitchen next to each other until it grew dark. We did not turn on the light, and we did not drink or talk; we sat quietly for a long time. Eventually she placed her hand lightly on my sleeve and told me that I should take logs up to the balcony room before too long.

When I went back to the balcony room no one was there except Bella who was still sitting at the end of the table. I piled the logs at each side of the hearth, using some of the smaller and drier ones to revitalize the dying embers. I drew the curtains and put on the lights.

"You have drugs, Thomas?" I heard her voice behind me and it was sharp and tense.

"You know I do not," I said.

"You will go to the town for me?"

"Impossible," I said, "because of the snow."

"It is not bad yet, Thomas, but soon you must go. You must help me."

Striding towards her I took her firmly by the shoulders.

"It is impossible, impossible to get to the town," I said. "You must understand that it is impossible."

As I looked at her I realized that she was as shocked at being touched as I was to find myself touching her. Always, always in the past I would have made great efforts to avoid this confrontation; I would not have spoken, I would not have entered the room, or having entered, quickly left. She looked at me and her eyes appealed for help. I told her that she must go to her room, lie down, be as calm as possible, put on more clothes.

She got up quietly and walked from the room, her arms hanging loosely at her sides.

By the time that we gathered in the balcony room to eat, the house was considerably warmer. Bella did not appear, nor of course Rebecca, so that we were a small group around the end of the table: Frieda, Nina, Elena, Genia, and myself. I was acutely conscious of the absence of Christina; in normal circumstances someone, usually Elena, would be serving her, telling her what had been placed before her—it is soup, and there is bread on the plate beside you.

Perhaps too they missed Maria, but it was impossible to be sure. They ate quickly, almost ravenously, and in silence. I got up and passed behind them, refilling their glasses, and occasionally putting more wood on the fire.

When we had finished eating Elena surprised me by asking suddenly if I had searched for Christina; I said that I had, and that I would explain in detail what had happened if she wished me to. But hearing myself make this offer I regretted it immediately because I knew that I did not want to talk to them about Christina. I could not understand why I had suggested such a thing. In any case I expected that Elena would not express further interest in my search, but on the contrary she asked me to tell my story, to tell it in all its detail. She listened intently as I spoke and did not take her eyes off me.

I told them about the rope, and the unseen animals that gnawed through it, about the giant ferns, the boulders, the height of the trees, the strange beauty of the green light in the forest that made me feel as if I was

under water. I told them then how I had thought that I
had seen her but that it turned out to be a fallen branch
covered with frozen snow. It was at this point that Genia
interrupted me, asking if I was sure that it was not her,
and had I looked beneath the snow?

For a moment her question seemed ridiculous,
because of course I had looked; but in fact I had not
looked carefully; I had not dug into the snow with my
bare hands and searched beneath it for her small body.
Instead, I had given it a swift glance, made an assump-
tion, and walked away. Genia was right, I could not be
absolutely certain that it was not her, and I realized
that as soon as possible I must return again to search
the forest. Had there been a clear sky, and if the moon
had been shining, if I had not felt so fatigued, then I
would have returned at that moment, spent the night
and the day and the night searching until inevitably I
found her; carried her to the truck, put her curled
frozen form on the seat beside me, carried her into the
house, placed her gently in front of the fire into which
I now stared...

"Thomas, come with me. Come to my room." It was
Frieda standing over me, demanding my attention. For
the first time I noticed that she was walking unsteadily
with the aid of a stick. As we passed through the door I
naturally took her elbow to guide and support her.

In her room she indicated that I should sit in the
usual chair while she fetched the brown bottle and two
glasses. As she sat down she sighed deeply. Her breathing was quick and shallow as if she was ill or in pain.

"A great deal of time has been wasted." As she talked
she began to play chess, leaning forward over the board

and studying the pieces closely. It seemed an attempt to make her words seem casual, though I was aware that I was being reproved.

"There are things that must be done," she continued. "There must be no more shirking of responsibilities."

"You seem to imply that there is some kind of time limit," I said.

"Thomas, look about you. Everything is in the grip of this fearful winter, but it will not last forever. The spring will come. All things will change."

"What must change?" I asked her.

"All things, Thomas; Genia is becoming a woman, Nina hankers after the world, I am an old woman... and Rebecca; day after day her illness gains ground and nothing is done to help her. Will you let her die, will you let such a vital life slip slowly through your fingers?"

"What can I do for Rebecca, how can I save Rebecca..."

"Go to her and discover this, Thomas. Go there, sit there, talk and wait until you find the answer." And she brought her clenched fist down hard on the chess board so that the pieces flew in every direction. She seemed suddenly humbled, as if ashamed of her outburst and she went to the cupboard to replenish our glasses. I went down on my knees and picked up the pieces and re-arranged them back on the board in the positions as I remembered them.

"But first," she continued, "you know that we must get Bella cured of her addiction, otherwise all your good work will be wasted and destroyed. She is a great danger to us at this time."

"We once tried to cure her, but failed."

"This time you must succeed. There is no other choice. You cannot get to the town and she cannot last out much longer in her present state of mind. Prepare yourself, Thomas, and of course we will help you. But do it soon, do it at once."

"I will give it all my attention," I assured her.

"And Thomas, you know that Genia has moved into Maria's room. I want you to move up out of the basement into the studio very soon. I want you up here, nearer to us. But you will have to accept that Elena is completing Christina's work and doing some painting of her own, and therefore she must be able to have use of the studio whenever she wants."

I nodded, but I did not reply as I got up and left the room. The idea of having Christina's room as my own was very pleasing to me, but the idea that I could share it with Elena was quite ridiculous. I would have no privacy, nowhere I could shut the door on myself and be alone. I would quietly ignore this order of Frieda's and stay put in my own dark room next to the kitchen.

Having left Frieda, I wandered the house. From the balcony room I saw that the sky was again clear and that therefore there would be another hard frost. I mulled over in my mind what Frieda had said to me, her conviction that all was changing and that time was limited; these thoughts I found stimulating. But her implication that I could be directly involved in helping Rebecca simply confused me; and her demand that I take charge of Bella's cure filled me with a sense of dread.

Many years before, Bella had asked for help to give up the drugs, but the attempt had failed and now I could no longer remember precisely what had gone wrong. I knew that hers was an addiction of the mind rather than of the body, and that a cure meant the precipitation of a crisis that would in itself break the habit, just as an animal is broken and just as behavior is changed by revolution. One sequence of events needed to be halted, and after a pause, another begun. First she must be allowed to take herself to the brink of destruction, herself and everything about her, but she must be restrained from the act itself, held back from the abyss. She must be allowed to exhaust herself, and to weather a crisis in safety.

In the kitchen I uncorked a few bottles of wine and diluted them with water in case I should need them; I placed them in a box and pushed it under my bed.

As I lay on my bed I calculated the number of days that she had either been without drugs or on a much reduced dose. Certainly she would be unable to hold out much longer. I was suprised that I found myself quite determined to succeed at this, as if I had a particular desire to please Frieda, or else to demonstrate to her that there was time, ample time.

In the morning I intended to go to Christina's room, the studio, but at the door I stopped, afraid for a moment of what I might feel if I went in. Inside nothing had been disturbed, everything was exactly as it had been on the night that she had fled except that the rope had been removed from the leg of the cupboard and thrown into a waste paper basket.

I sat in the chair in the window and adjusted the mirror so that I could see most of the room, including the chair on which she so often sat to work on the sculpture.

I wondered what had been said to her that had made her so frightened of me on that day, what had so totally changed her feelings from friendship to fear.

I began to wander about the room, picking up and holding objects of hers, touching things that she had touched only a few days ago; lying on her bed, closing my eyes and listening to the sounds that she would have heard. Sound from the heating pipes, the continuous sound of the wind against the windows that overlooked the river, some other muffled noises from within the house. I realized how solitary she must have felt, how confined and held within this one room; how with memory and touch and imagination she recreated an entire world, a world in which for most of the time she seemed so content.

Elena entered the room and closed the door behind her before she caught sight of me lying on the bed.

"Thomas, I am sorry, I thought that you had not yet moved in. I will come back later." And she turned to leave the room.

I got to my feet quickly and assured her that I had not moved in, that I probably would not do so, and asked her to carry on with whatever she wanted to do. After a moment's hesitation she sat down before the sculpture and pulled off the plastic cover, revealing her own image.

For a few minutes she sat immobile before it, her hands in her lap, scrutinizing the clay form with an intense gaze. And as she did not seem to expect me to leave, nor show any signs of being perturbed by my presence, I took a book from the shelf and sat down again in the window seat. When at last she began to

work on the sculpture I quietly turned my chair away
from the window and the mirror, and watched her
directly.

She sat straight backed, holding her head very still,
her long fingers moving the clay precisely; and she
worked presumably from memory because there was
no mirror nor photograph near her. Curiously I felt no
sense of discomfort as I watched her; and nor when I
let my gaze move slowly over her was this scrutiny in
any way crude or analytical. The inner voice spoke its
lines word by word as if to slow down the movement
of my eyes and bring about a deepening of my concentration; and the voice spoke tenderly.... the eyelids
closing so quickly over the beautiful eyes; and why are
the eyes particularily beautiful, because they shine,
because of the strong brow, because of strength, intelligence; or because of a sense of sexuality held in check,
or even denied. Or was it all in my own mind; I
wanted her to like me, I feared her, I dared not desire
her, considered her inhuman as if she had literally not
been born on earth.

And nor was I oblivious of the fact that she sat in
Christina's chair and worked at Christina's sculpture;
that she had slept with her, and yet betrayed her.

Yet in essence, they were much alike; that is, I experienced the same longings and the same desires. But
whereas with Christina there had always been the
chance, the remote chance of escape and fulfilment,
with Elena no such idea could be imagined. Despite her
strength and beauty and elegance, she was always
unknowable, always a stranger, always in the end unreliable and too fragile to be touched.

She suddenly returned my stare and her face gave not a single clue as to what she thought or felt. When she spoke her tone of voice was almost intimate.

"You know Thomas, that I would give you lessons, teach you to draw and sculpt. I think it is what you wanted. If you moved into this room it would be very convenient and easy."

"Yes," I said. "I will give it some thought."

"When will you move here?"

"Tomorrow. Probably tomorrow," I replied.

She returned to her work on the sculpture, and I to my pretended reading of the book in my lap. Later I replaced the book on the shelf and left the room as quietly as possible.

I had not spoken to Rebecca since my return, so I made my way to her room. Frieda's irritation or anger still nagged at my mind and I wanted to see if simply sitting with Rebecca, being in her presence, would give any clue as to how I could possibly be instrumental in her salvation. The idea was purely experimental; I was quite sure that nothing would occur.

As I sat on the edge of the bed she stirred slightly and opened her eyes for a split second, enough I felt to reassure herself that she had assumed correctly the identity of the person who sat by her. She took my hand and gripping it tightly, drew it down under the sheet and held it there.

Thinking that I must this time make the effort to talk, I decided to recount the story that I had told on the previous evening, the story of my search in the forest for Christina. I spoke slowly and unwittingly embellished the story; the boulders glowed in the green light, Christina's spirit hid itself first behind one tree and then another, and she cut the rope in many places, and out of sight, she laughed at me; she hoped that I would have faith in her, believe her, be tempted by her; be lost with her in the forest and embrace a strange new world wholeheartedly...

And when the hand that Rebecca clutched had long since gone numb, my rambling story led me on to hope that I, Thomas, could save her, Rebecca, from her tragic and unbearable fate—the inexorable slide into masculinity. I simply wanted to feel that there was something that I could do.

She began to move, almost to squirm in the bed, and it was a moment before I understood that she wanted to sit up. I adjusted the pillows and lifted her as best I could. As she lay there, breathing deeply, her eyes still shut, I realized how weak she had become, what a great effort it was for her to raise the energy to say even a few words.

But before she was able to speak to me the door burst open and Genia came quickly into the room. Rebecca's eyes opened; she recognized who it was, and something like a smile formed briefly on her gray lips. Genia embraced me elaborately and announced that she had come to give Rebecca her massage. She pushed me back into a chair a short distance from the bed, insisting that I stay, saying that while she did the work, I could do the talking. But I was much too interested in Genia's massage to be able to say anything.

She first uncovered one of Rebecca's legs, poured on some oil, and rubbed it in vigorously and professionally. She then raised and bent and stretched the limb, moving it in the air almost as if it danced. This she repeated with the other leg and then with both of her arms. She turned Rebecca onto her front and completely pulled the bedclothes off her and removed her nightgown; she oiled, massaged, and pummeled the sallow skin of her back and the pale dimpled flesh of her buttocks. And during this process Rebecca farted several times, and I saw when she faced me that she dribbled profusely into the pillow. But the enjoyment that she derived from Genia's manipulations was amazing to see, expressed simply by the complete absence of pain and sadness from her face, but also by her eyes which seemed to roll with pleasure behind the closed lids.

I was amazed too by Genia's attitude, the confidence and efficiency with which she dealt with Rebecca; the fact that there was no hint that she found the task irksome or unpleasant, and indeed every indication that she enjoyed it as much as her patient.

Having turned Rebecca again onto her back she carefully replaced her nightgown and covered her up, arranging the bedclothes neatly about her. She kissed Rebecca and kissed me, and as quickly as she had arrived she left the room, telling us that she and Nina intended to clear all the snow from the balcony.

I did not move from my chair. I saw that Rebecca seemed to return at once to her normal state, neither awake or asleep. I was disappointed that the massage had such a short-lived beneficial effect. Perhaps she was improved, or at least prevented from declining further; but perhaps Genia had wasted her time, and perhaps I wasted mine.

Sitting there I allowed myself to be overwhelmed by a sense of irritation with the situation; bored and angered by the fact that she lay, day after day, half dead, half alive; and though tended by us all, seemed so incapable of helping herself. Why did she not try to raise herself to her feet. Why was it necessary to be such a gruesome burden, and such a damn weight on my mind?

I knew in that moment that I could stand it no more, that I would be unable to return to the room again, or think of her again, the hair on her thighs, the vacant eyes, the vacant sickly mouth. I leapt to my feet with the clear intention of leaving the room at once; in my mind I heard the door slamming behind me, intending to indicate and always remind her that I had washed my hands of her forever...

But to my astonishment I found myself kneeling by the bed gathering the weight of her head and shoulders into my arms. I leant forward and kissed her; a long passionate kiss with the feeling that around us nothing else existed, no sound, no other life. When I lowered her back onto her pillows her eyes were wide open and I knew then that I had no idea what her reaction might be; perhaps, if she could, she would scream. But the expression in her eyes was not wild or frightened, but quite calm. There was also a new expression on her lips and I thought perhaps this was merely the impression left by our kiss. If such a face could be eloquent, then it said, *So at last you have decided to kiss me.*

And I answered this question aloud, saying, *Yes.* She did not relapse into sleep as I had expected, but continued to regard me with her strange new expression and her level, passive gaze. I told her that I would see her on the next day, and I got up from my knees and went away.

I returned to my room in a daze, mumbling to myself that, of course, though her skin was cold to the touch, nevertheless after a few moments one felt the warmth emerging; that so often I forgot this, forgot too that she would always listen attentively to my deepest thoughts and allow my deepest feelings; that she required of me so little, and granted endlessly as much as she was able, her gift of time.

As I opened the door to my room and turned on the light I saw Bella on all fours rummaging under my bed. Her black limbs were long and thin, too thin. She spat out that she was searching for the drugs. I told her again that I had none. She kicked out at the box that was under the bed and quickly darted for the door and made her escape, as if she feared that I might strike her.

Nine

Bella was curled up on her bed, her hands clasped about her knees. She did not move or speak as I entered her room. I searched quickly, looking for anything that might be dangerous; glasses, sharp objects, knives, needles. I pulled the curtains to darken the room. Kneeling before her I could see the effects of the withdrawal on her face; its tension and strange pallor, the way in which the eyes seemed so deep set.

"Thomas." She opened her eyes and looked at me directly. "I have to tell you this; my face aches and my teeth and my ears and my head. My legs and arms are in pain. But it is my stomach that is in agony..."

"Yes, I understand," I said. "But will you succeed?"

"Yes, but do not leave me, Thomas, for god's sake stay close by."

"I will," I replied. "I will be outside the door. If you want wine or anything, then you only have to bang on the door. You understand? And I will lock you in, you agree?"

"Yes, yes." And as she spoke her hand shot out and clenched hard at my wrist. I waited, and her eyes closed and her hand relaxed its grip and released me.

As I left I took the key from the door and locked it behind me. On the landing outside her room there was a small table and I brought a chair and placed it by this. When in late afternoon it began to grow dark I turned on the electric light; but I found this much too bright and went quickly for a candle stick and a supply of the valuable candles. I sat there quietly in the flickering light, waiting and listening.

On one occasion Nina brought me coffee, and on another Genia came and sat on the table, swinging her legs. She was anxious about what might befall Bella and I reassured her that I would not sleep until I knew that she was safe. She did not stay for long. From the room there was no sound except for the occasional, barely audible sighing or moaning.

At about the middle of the evening I heard a faint tapping at the door and I quickly unlocked it. She was standing just inside the door, a forlorn figure, her hands hanging down at her sides, her hair a wild mess. She asked me to help her change her clothes and she returned to the bed and sat down. Maneuvering her arms and legs as best I could, I undressed her; under her shirt and dress she wore no underclothes, and I could see that every part of her body glistened with sweat. I asked her what she wanted to put on and she replied that anything would do, anything I wanted; from the wardrobe I chose a long, loose crimson robe probably made of silk and probably one that I had seen her wearing recently. I sent this billowing over her head, and pulled her arms through the sleeves. She shifted to the center of the bed, at once bringing up her knees and spreading her legs in a natal position; placing her hands flat on her belly, she let out a long cry of pain. When I approached her she told me to get out, to get out quickly...

Perhaps I dozed, perhaps I entered a dream. I awoke to hear, or convinced myself that I had just heard an unfamiliar noise. Realizing that I must at once unlock the door to see what was happening, I attempted to reach for the key that I had placed on the table beside me; but I could not move my arm. At first I assumed that for some reason it had gone numb, but I soon knew that I could not move any of my limbs, not my hands, nor fingers, nor even the tongue in my mouth to call out. I was paralyzed, and though my brain strained and urged my body to act, there was nothing that I could do. And as I sat there I began to feel an icy draft blowing over my body, making my eyes water and my skin feel dead.

I prayed that someone might pass along the landing but realized that they might not do so for hours. I thought that by an effort of will I could somehow fling myself from the chair and that the impact would wake up my body, or the noise attract attention. But all movement was impossible.

Gradually I calmed myself, stopped the panic that was rising in me. I thought of Bella, of the sweat pouring from her skin, of the metal orb inside her, of the fact that she might be lying injured, a self-inflicted wound pouring forth blood. I imagined her face, and she was smiling, an evil smile that bared her teeth; the face came closer and closer to mine and the tongue voiced my name, and she began to laugh in my face; her lips pursed to spit at me. Summoning every atom of strength in my body, I raised my hand and lashed her hard across the side of her face... and in that moment the spell was broken and I could at last move; my hand swung hard against the candlestick on the table beside me and sent it flying along the landing.

I unlocked the door to her room and flung open the door. I was met by a blast of freezing air. Snow was billowing in through the wide-open window. A crude rope of knotted sheets led from the radiator and out through the window and down the side of the house to within a few yards of the ground. There were marks in the snow where she had jumped. As quickly as I could I heaved the sheet rope back into the room and slammed the window shut. As I ran from the room I met Nina on the landing, staring at me and holding the candlestick that she had picked up from the floor. I shouted to her to come with me, to tell Frieda what had happened, to get the others to come and help us.

I assumed for some reason that she would have made for the river, but on that side of the house there was no sign of her. I went a little way in the direction of the cove, but it was clear that she was not there. I could not see far in the driving snow and a weak moonlight only occasionally broke through the somber sky, so that for much of the time I had to search closely on my hands and knees for her footprints. But as I turned to go

to the back of the house I heard the truck revving violently and realized at once what she would try to do.

I was in time to see the truck lurch forward and then
roar away wildly in the direction of the scrub-land; but
at the same time I knew that she was well off the track
and would not get far. Suddenly the front of the truck
dipped sharply as the front wheels went into a deep
drift and the vehicle could go no further. There was a
screeching of gears as she tried desperately to find
reverse. Then the engine stalled and within a few
moments all was quiet; only the sound of my feet in the
snow, some noises from the house, and the wind gust-
ing and dying away, whistling about the rough hewn
stone of the house.

As I trudged towards the truck I heard voices behind
me near to the house; Nina certainly, and Genia; and
perhaps Elena. When I was within a few yards of the
truck the cab door suddenly flew open and Bella's body
fell from the seat and hung there upside down as if she
was trapped by the feet. I rushed forward and began to
lift her, and within a few moments Nina was by my side
helping me.

We managed to get her free and down onto the snow;
but as I was about to pick her up to carry her back to the
house, she leapt at me and tried to grab at my throat.
There was a distorted and hideous expression on her
face so that I believed that she had gone mad. Nina fled,
and I defended myself, fighting her off while trying not
to strike her, falling back into the snow, trying to stop
her while at the same time trying to avoid her thrashing
arms and legs, her teeth and her nails; the strength and
fury of the attack were phenomenal, beyond belief.

With the same speed with which she had launched her attack, she suddenly pulled back from me; clutching at her belly, she let out a terrifying scream. She fell back into the snow, still holding herself, screaming once more before lying quiet and motionless.

I too lay there for some time, breathing deeply, slowly recovering from the assault. Her first scream so close to my face had hurt my ears, and the second, though I was in some way prepared for it, had entered my head, the very center of my brain and filled me with a terrible dread, a sense of absolute terror. Perhaps in that moment had I been able to raise myself, had I been alone, then I would have killed her; with a knife, with my bare hands...

Nina and Genia came to me and helped me to my feet; and then Nina went to look at Bella. I told Genia that I was all right and that I wanted her to close the door of the truck and to turn off the ignition. As I watched her do this I saw Elena standing near to the wall of the house; she seemed frightened and lost, her back to the stone, her hands spread out along each side of her as if for support. She did not approach, but she watched intently all that occurred.

As I lifted Bella her arms moved gently up around my neck and her face, now placid, rested against my chest. Her breathing was shallow and I could barely hear her when she spoke.

"The child, Thomas, the child is coming."

There was snow in her eyebrows and in her hair; her body felt cold and hard, and I could feel her bones as if she were starved. I could feel the tension, the awful force within her that was not yet spent, not yet exorcized.

As I began to carry her awkwardly through the snow, I began to doubt that the battle could be won; I was exhausted, defeated, and I wanted only to sleep. I was thinking about my dark sanctuary near to the kitchen, my days in the cabin; of simplicity and order, of emotions weaving through life like a gentle meandering river, cool and predictable, essentially contained and controlled. Even as I climbed the stairs with her I was inventing a dream in which I was no longer a prisoner, no longer a victim, no longer myself.

(In the dream I put her down on the stairs in a sitting position against the balustrades. I took her slender hands and curled the fingers about the woodwork, and supported her head between the posts. She seemed presentable; that is, it did not seem that she had been abandoned...)

I put her down on the bed in her room. The others were nowhere to be seen and I wondered why I had failed to notice that they had disappeared. Soon afterwards Frieda came through the open door, walking slowly, leaning heavily on her stick.

"Is it over?" She asked.

But before I had time to reply, Bella flew from the bed, seeming to hurl her whole body against Frieda, before collapsing onto the floor. Frieda's body buckled at the knees and I managed to catch her so that she did not fall heavily; there were four deep scratch marks across her face, and the blood was on the point of flowing.

On the landing I yelled out for Nina and Elena and when they arrived they lifted Frieda, who was pale and shocked, and carried her from the room; the scratches were now red streaks and there was blood pouring down onto the white material of her blouse.

I lifted Bella, but now her body was heavy and lifeless. I laid her again on the bed and very slowly she uncurled herself, and then equally slowly resumed the natal posture. She was moaning and whimpering to herself. Her hands groped pathetically at her flat stomach and there were bruises beginning to appear on her knees and ankles and arms.

I had no reason to really believe it, but I felt certain that now the worst was past, that the violence was over. I felt strangely peaceful. I wanted a drink, but I dare not go to get one. I lay down on the pile of cushions near to the bed and I closed my eyes and listened to her breathing.

After a while she began to speak, the words coming slowly, sometimes vicious in tone, sometimes almost tender. It was a form of dirge, a chant, both loud and soft, and when its tone changed it seemed to parallel spasms of pain that occasionally still passed through her body. It was abuse, or meant to be abuse, and it hurt me that she wished it so; but I seemed incapable of denying or verifying the truth or not of the abuse and I thought perhaps that though she used my name, she actually spoke about another. Or else that she described me, but as I had been before, even a few hours before, and not as I had now become. But I did not cease to listen; I allowed it to wash around me, waves that sometimes burned me and sometimes froze me, and sometimes were not felt at all.

"You are like a dog, Thomas, a dog on its hind legs... a dog on its hind legs... wearing red trousers and a green shirt... displaying yourself, running round and round the ring, so proud of yourself... showing off your underside with pride... running and strutting in order to stay upright... even when the horses thunder in the ring or the trapeze artist leaps through the air, still running round and round, confident that you are the center of attention, the center of the world... a dog, dressed in green and red, strutting on its hind legs..."

As I listened to her voice I fell into a dream, allowing my mind to visualize the images that she seemed to create. I hardly noticed when Elena came back into the room, closing the door quietly behind her; presumably she had taken care of Frieda, taken her to her room, bathed her wounds. She stood still for several minutes listening I suppose to what Bella was saying; and I was quite sure, since everything was calm, that she would return to her own room. But instead she came and lay down on the cushions next to me. She lay on her back very close to me and stared passively at the ceiling. After a few moments she took my hand and held it loosely.

The voice of Bella continued, though perhaps she spoke more quietly.

"Thomas, poor, sad, dirty, Thomas, dogmatic Thomas, the dogma of meanness, inelegance, unpleasantness... the dogma of inflexibility, opinion, war, justice, opinion, and more war... poor Thomas, insensitive, fearful, obsessed, hypocritical, devious, deceitful, shallow, Thomas, devoid of poetry and mystery and love of life, devoid of vision... a dry dog, a gristle-dog, an unclean dog..."

At those moments when I registered an involuntary reaction to what she said, I am sure that Elena's grip tightened slightly on my hand. At one point I almost got up because I feared that Bella might leap up again from the bed, but Elena restrained me; perhaps she misunderstood and thought that I rose up because I could no longer tolerate Bella's words; perhaps she thought that I might strike her.

"Dog-like... dog-cheap... dogged... doggy-paddling... dog-shit Thomas..."

Later Genia came into the room; did she feel alone, did she seek company, warmth. She came to lie with us on the cushions, but to my surprise did not choose to lie down on the other side of Elena, but squeezed sleepily into the narrow space between myself and the wall; without moving closer to Elena I could make no more room for her. She faced me, her eyes hardly open, curled her body slightly and went to sleep at once.

"...crude, uncultured dog-like-dog... pretending to be the dog-like top dog... dog eats dog... duels, death, dogs... When the sun shine, dog in the manger... when the wind blows, violence and death, pleasure and dirt... how do you hold your head up... why do you live... Free of the dog we could run, leap, shout, sing, yell, live like the wind in freedom and joy... Bastard dog, you stink, you stink, you stink... damn dog, damn you dog..."

As I listened I saw the door open very slowly and a figure dressed in a white nightgown enter the room; the figure shuffled on its feet, turned on the spot, found it difficult to keep balance, closed the door with great difficulty. It was Rebecca. I sat upright and watched her. She moved very slowly to the other side of the bed and sat down on the edge. She placed a shaking hand on Bella's brow; and at once she was silenced, the dreadful monologue was halted.

Elena, concerned for Rebecca perhaps, got up from her place beside me and went and knelt on the floor between the two women; Genia also woke and went to sit on the end of Bella's bed to see what was happening.

They did not move, not a muscle; there was an uncanny stillness about them all.

I was able to watch them for what seemed like an eternity. Bella's black hair against the white of the pillow, and the red of her robe against the white of Rebecca's nightgown; Rebecca's heavy, pale face framed by the abundance and redness of her hair; the slender pale neck and pale face of Elena, her fair hair in a single plait that curled on her shoulder, the end tied in a small black scarf; Genia, her brown trousers and shirt, her bare feet, a single gold ring on her finger, her brown eyes fixed on Bella.

For a long time I observed the beauty and strangeness of these women; the image was beyond comprehension; their uniqueness, yet the strength of the bond that so clearly united them. I experienced a sense of absolute exclusion, hopeless, inevitable exclusion; and also a sense of longing, a desire and a pain. The desire to know, the pain of endless unknowing. I wondered, if I abandoned desire, would I also be free of pain. But then I could not consider this; I was at last uncertain of everything. And in any case the thought was irrelevant; I had only recently discovered this new desire, this painful hunger for the human spirit, and I was not prepared yet to give it up.

Eventually Elena and Genia helped Rebecca back to her room. I was alone again with Bella who was now quiet, though her eyes were not closed. I lay back on the cushions. As if abandoning myself to sleep, I allowed my mind to be flooded by pure emotion; I was surprised and curious to find that I was smiling. I assumed at first that this was because I was so pleased and amazed that Rebecca had been able to get from her bed and come to Bella's room; but it was not this.

My pleasure came from an overwhelming sense of relief, not that I had ignored or forgotten all that Bella had said during the night; on the contrary I remembered it well, understood what she meant, knew when she exaggerated and knew when she was correct in her judgment. But I knew also that I was not condemned by these accusations because I had discovered that I was able to change. What had seemed an absolute and rigid vision was now crumbling. Anything was possible. Everything was now new and fascinating. I recognized that in the beginning most things were neutral, benign, natural; and were only made crude or sick or wrong by the malice and envy and meanness that I projected onto them.

If I had not been acutely aware of Bella's presence, if I had been less tired, then my smile might have turned into outright laughter, joyous laughter, overriding embarrassed laughter about the dog who lay severely shaken, on his pile of cushions, his green shirt all torn, his red trousers in tatters.

When I awoke it was not quite daylight. I had rolled over against the wall and I was covered by a blanket. The sheet rope had been all untied, and Bella had also been covered. I stood over her. She appeared to be in a deep sleep, and her face was relaxed and peaceful. It was a fine, strong face. With the tips of my fingers I touched it and found the texture of the skin incredibly soft and cool. I touched her lips. I let a finger run along the cicatrix, and the sense of fragility there and its tension engendered a powerful sensation that permeated my entire body; it was as if the cells of my body remembered the blood, the pain, and were aroused again to a pitch of passion.

Watching for a few moments longer to ensure that she was well asleep and that I had not disturbed her, I left the room and went down to the basement. I stayed long enough only to shower and change my clothes.

When I returned to her room I found Nina on the landing with a tray of coffee, unsure whether or not she should disturb Bella. I offered to take the tray in and as I took it from her, without thinking I leant forward to kiss her. But she moved her head sharply away from me and avoided my lips. Once she was sure that I had hold of the tray she walked away quickly towards the stairs.

Suddenly it was as if my new state of mind, my new strength could be destroyed by a simple rejection; the old anger surfaced within me. I put down the tray on the small table and sat on the chair. I recalled sitting there on the previous evening; I recalled the events of the night. I spoke aloud to myself; Nina had merely expressed herself, and it was the wish not to be kissed; nothing else was known. My reaction had been that of the dog on hind legs.

As I opened the door I saw that Frieda was sitting by the bed, caressing and stroking the hand that had scratched her. I went to fetch another cup, and then sat on a chair in the window while they talked in whispers. Finally Bella held out her hand to me, and I came forward to take it. Frieda adjusted the sheets around her, and Bella turned her head on the pillow and closed her eyes. Frieda asked me to go back with her to her room.

Once there she climbed with difficulty onto the four-poster and ensconced herself amidst a pile of pillows.

"I suppose," she said, "that it would not appeal to you to embrace an old woman?"

I smiled and leant towards her across the bed.

"No, no, Thomas, come up here and put your arm around me properly." So I climbed onto the bed beside her and half sitting up against the pillows, I put my arm around her. Her head lay against my chin; she seemed to smell of coffee and of log fires; her short hair was sharp against my skin.

"Promise me, Thomas, that you will forget almost at once what I am about to say to you."

"I promise," I said.

"You have done well this night."

"There seems to be no doubt that she is cured," I said.

"Ah, Thomas, it is certainly good that she came to no harm, but you know perfectly well that Bella's cure was not the main business of the night. The dangerous addiction was yours, and it was about you that we were mainly concerned."

I thought for a few moments about what she had said; yes, of course, it was I who had been tested, the crisis had been mine. It seemed to me then that Bella had offered herself as a sacrifice; that things might not have been as they were, that indeed I might have harmed her.

I looked down again at the scratches on Frieda's face, the red wounds outlined by the ridge of white swollen flesh. I asked her if the scratches still hurt, and she replied that they did not hurt any more.

"I will sleep now, Thomas," she said.

I kissed her on the forehead and eased my arm out from behind her. I pulled the curtains closed around the bed.

As I was leaving the room I noticed that the books which lay open on the arrangement of tables in the middle of the room seemed to have been changed in some way. On looking more closely I saw that the figures on the pages were not hieroglyphs, nor ideograms, but were minute line drawings, some very subtly shaded in pale colors.

I felt that I could interpret these symbols and in one place almost read the line; there was a river, a house, some people, and over the page no doubt I would find the action or the event, the meaning therefore. But as I tried to turn the page my sleeve caught one of the mousetraps and it slammed shut with a loud bang.

I heard Frieda's drowsy voice from behind the curtain of the bed.

"Be off with you now, Thomas. Go to bed."

I left the room and went to the studio to sleep.

Ten

Since I planned to be outside for some considerable time I dressed as warmly as possible and pushed one of the bottles of diluted wine into the pocket of my top-coat.

First I went to inspect the massive pieces of ice that had destroyed the jetty. There were signs that they had melted slightly; they were now thicker at the bottom than at the top, and pieces of wood and old rope were partially exposed. I assumed that sometimes, probably at about midday, the temperature had risen above freezing and the ice had melted a little. But by mid-afternoon the temperature was again below freezing. The same was true of the snow. The depth everywhere of between a yard and half a yard seemed to be a constant; sometimes during the day the top few inches were melted, but during the night it snowed again.

At the cove I had the impression that the level of the water in the river had dropped. This was difficult to judge since there was always a small tide—the effect of the moon and the winds. But if as I suspected, the water level had actually fallen, then this was an ominous sign because it meant that many hundreds of miles to the east at the head-waters, the lakes and springs were frozen; and that therefore even at this late stage in the year, there must still be snow on the mountains. It also meant that the toxic filth in the river would tend to become more concentrated as the flow diminished.

Lying down between the two old boats that had been pulled up on the sand above the cove, I was able to shelter somewhat from the biting wind. It saddened me that the river had no calm, quiet periods, but was always like a river in flood—muddied, with no vegetation at its banks, no trees, no plants, nothing but dead, blackened soil and stone. It surged monotonously, relentlessly, a giant sewer, it being important only that it should reach the sea as soon as possible.

It angered me, anger that became almost immediately an impotent despair. Cursed river, cursed people. There was nothing mysterious about the state of the river, it was not an act of God and to pray for some change seemed inappropriate. The pollution was the result of a rational, easily understood sequence of events; the mind of man could be changed. I was not certain whether or not I should take some comfort from the fact that I now felt this depth of despair, whereas before it had concerned me only when it affected me directly, only when I noticed, only when I remembered how beautiful it had been.

I took a long drink from the bottle but was forced to spit it out at once. The water that I had used to dilute the wine was salty. Therefore the well was tainted again; as soon as the weather improved I must clean the tanks and replace all the filters.

Looking at the boat against which I was sitting, I considered the possibility of drifting down the river to the town in order to collect essential supplies; our food was now being severely rationed, and fuel for the truck and the chain saw were low. But even if this had been possible it would have necessitated a long march back carrying the supplies on our backs. A long, arduous trek in the snow; myself, Nina, Genia; no, not Genia. Nina and myself. It was obviously pointless and impossible. We must eat less, one meal a day, and pray that the weather soon changed.

I got to my feet and continued my wandering. I had the feeling of not having taken this walk for a long time; or indeed, as if I walked it for the first time. Not only had my feelings about the river changed, but I also realized that I could now bear to recall vivid memories of times at the cove or when using the boats, and the recollection gave me pleasure. Even the misplaced cherry orchard seemed to me to have a stark beauty; the sturdy trunks of the trees, the bark peeling to reveal the redness beneath, the snow on their outspread branches, the symmetry with which they had been planted.

It was here, on the edge of the cherry orchard that I met Elena, and she turned and walked back to the house with me. She questioned me in detail about the weather; when I thought the thaw might come, and what we should do if it did not. I did not try to hide from her that

I felt the situation to be serious, that I felt the severity of the weather to be both unusual and alarming.

At the house we did something which in the following days we would repeat very often; something that afforded me greater and greater pleasure, a ritual that I looked forward to with a feeling bordering on excitement. It was simply that we sat alone together in the balcony room by the window, overlooking the balcony and the river, slowly sipping brandy and talking. Perhaps it was the brandy that provided the opportunity to speak and be silent as the mood took us; or perhaps it was that we thought we conducted a vigil, patiently watching the sky and the river for signs of change; on guard, alert for the first indication that winter was giving way to spring.

We talked of all kinds of things, gleaning little by little greater knowledge, and therefore greater understanding of each other. She talked at length and in detail about the village where she was born and as I concentrated and tried to imagine the scene, I watched the movement of the river at the end of the sand bar–the way in which it swirled and eddied, forming a small whirlpool.

Later, whenever I caught sight of the sand bar, or the whirlpool, or sat in this same chair in the window, I instantly recalled what she had so clearly described: the village square, the trees, the café, the shops, the children on bicycles, the fountain, the women at the fountain. And I would enter the square and my mind would fill with questions as if I had to be convinced beyond all doubt that such places had existed, might exist still; and also questions about her, the young girl in the square.

Which fruit did she buy, and from which shop, and as she ate, what had she thought, what had she felt?

It was as impossible to describe the wonderful sensation of sitting there with her, as it was to account for the fact that she seemed equally engrossed, equally contented; it seemed that she enjoyed, even took reassurance from my company.

During the days that followed all kind of changes took place in the house, yet at the same time there was a calm and order, almost a routine to the life.

Every morning early I went for my walk which was also a tour of inspection—across the sand bar, around the cove and beyond, returning to the house via the cherry orchard. More often than not I would encounter Bella somewhere near to the cove where she was beachcombing for objects that she could use in her prayers. She said that she prayed for the arrival of spring. She prayed also for Christina, that she might not suffer solitude, that in paradise the gods gave her comfort. Since I now slept in the studio, I was able to give her a number of small objects that had belonged to Christina for use in her ritual remembrance. Though I believed little that Bella said, nevertheless I listened intently and savored every word that she spoke concerning Christina; I permitted myself a great and secret indulgence, the hope, almost a faith in the idea that Christina might still be alive.

Though I had moved my few possessions into the studio, I did not entirely give up the room in the basement; sometimes in the night I would go there, light a candle, take out her photograph from my wallet. It was

a morbid act, something from the past, no longer wor-
thy of my new life; yet I could not entirely give it up.

Afterwards I tended always to be angry with myself.
I felt it to be a negative act, almost a sin, and that one
day I would be punished. And at the same time I knew
now that I could talk about these feelings; to Nina, or
Frieda perhaps, or Rebecca, or even to Elena; and that
in their different ways they would forbid and dispel this
fantasy, banish the indulgence, the self-abasement from
my life. But I could not yet bear to part with it, would
not confess and abandon it.

Whenever I drove the truck to the forest edge to collect logs, I also gave some time to the search. I
unwound the rope as before, and sometimes in quiet
desperation I would dare to go beyond its length,
deeper into the forest. Particularly I searched for the
fallen branch covered with snow that Genia had
reminded me about. No doubt I failed to find exactly
the same one, but I dug into tangled mounds of branch
and fern and snow in the vain hope that I would find
her body curled beneath. The loss of Christina continued to haunt and to spoil my new life.

At some point in each day I walked with Rebecca.
We walked very slowly and I supported her around the
shoulders, letting her lean on me. I had positioned
upright chairs at strategic places throughout the house,
at the foot of the stairs for example, so that when she
was tired she was able to rest almost immediately.
Sometimes she resisted the idea of this exercise, wanting
to stay in her bed and to sleep; but it was never difficult
to rouse her, and her progress from day to day was

remarkable. When some new target had been achieved, some greater number of paces, she would sit on the chair quietly chuckling to herself, and chiding me for being such a task master. And with her improvement in health and strength there was also in her a growing awareness of her own femininity, even her sexuality; and so great was her joy at the discovery of these feelings and sensations, that at times she became almost over-excited, somehow bullying me, but with endless charm. She sent me to steal, or to "obtain quietly" as she put it, some of Maria's underclothing, and I was to ensure that it was both attractive and sturdy.

The great triumph was our first walk in the open air; we walked the length of the balcony and sat for a few moments on the parapet. And though she still became very tired towards the end of the day, nevertheless she began sometimes to appear at meal times and to join in with the life of the house. I was disappointed that I could not get to the town to buy her the things that she wanted, and sad too that our meals had become so sparse and uninteresting. It seemed a pity that as her hunger for life increased day by day, the material quality of that life became gradually poorer.

At about mid-morning Elena came to the studio to continue her work on the sculpture. I quickly got used to her presence, and if I had nothing else to do I would often watch her as she worked, noticing that as time passed she became more relaxed. Her movements became freer, less precise, and she would sometimes wander the room or throw herself down in a chair, letting her legs dangle casually over the side.

Later in the morning, or else during the early evening, I sometimes joined Genia in the art lesson; particularly I wanted Elena to teach me to draw. I was keen to fathom the mystery whereby without apparently much thought, she was able so easily to transpose an object onto a piece of paper: a jug, a table, a bowl, a hand, or a face.

I was slow to learn; I only began to succeed in a small way when Elena began to correct my bad habits of thought. She would place her hand over mine which held the pencil and guide it smoothly as she observed the subject. My hand, contained and controlled in this way could do nothing but yield to her guidance; and my face, close to her breast, felt the warmth of her body as she showed me how to take risks, how to transform fear into a fluid creativity. But the fear that I could not eliminate was the fear that I would be unable to achieve these things, or feel these things, except in her presence. And that therefore I was bound to her, dependent on her, always in grave danger without her.

Elena herself spent many hours in Frieda's room; they sat close to each other studying the books that covered the tables. It seemed that Frieda was imparting to Elena all that she had learned about the texts. When I first knew about this I was aggrieved because I had always hoped that one day Frieda would show them to me; but since I was now so much closer to Elena this did not seem so important. As time passed they spent many more hours closeted together and I could not avoid the feeling that the intensity of their work suggested that there was some urgency.

It was apparent that Frieda was seriously ill; she was often silent or distracted, and she withdrew from the life of the house, often not appearing at meal times. As we sat one day drinking our brandy in the balcony room, I asked Elena about this illness, if she suffered pain, and what we could do about the situation. She described vague symptoms, implying that there was no specific disease but simply the aches and pains of age, made worse by the weather; there were medicines that she wanted me to collect as soon as it was possible to drive to the town. Meanwhile Frieda wanted only to rest so that she could put all her energy into the teaching.

As I thought again about the hellish persistence of the freeze, my eyes caught sight of the whirlpool beyond the sand bar and immediately my mind was filled with an image of the village and the village square that Elena had described to me. She smiled at this rapid change of subject as I asked her a question about herself at that time. In my imagination I saw her crossing the square carrying a basket; she wore a skirt that reached to the ground, but her splendid shoulders were uncovered and she called out something to a boy who was standing by the fountain. Therefore I asked Elena what it felt like to be that woman; what was it like literally to be within the skin of herself, to possess the hand that touched herself, to see herself in a mirror; and what was it like to look at the world with her eyes; and what was this world that she saw, how ugly, how beautiful, and of what duration.

She said that it was impossible to answer such questions, but I urged her to try. After some thought she got up and went to the door of the balcony room and beck-

oned me to follow her. In the studio she told me to lie
spread-eagled on the bed. When I had done this, she
carefully lay face upwards precisely on top of me, the
back of her head on my chin, her arms resting on my
arms, her legs balanced on mine. She said nothing, but
lay quite still. I could feel her weight, which was merely
a gentle pressure, and I could feel her breathing. What I
saw of the ceiling must have been almost identical to
her view; a swirling soft reflection of the falling snow
flakes. I felt the back of her hands in my hands, her
heels on the top of my feet, her buttock pressing into
my belly. Her perfect ears near to mine heard what I
heard, and she could make no movement that I did not
register.

Gradually my body seemed to become in tune with
hers; our breathing synchronized, our temperatures
equalized, and at the same time it was as if our thoughts
merged. It was as if we were one, or as if my body contained hers, her thoughts, sensations and feelings.

I do not think that I fell asleep but I entered a trance
in which I was changed in a way that is beyond comprehension; when I awoke she was gone. I lay still for some
time, gradually yielding to my feelings, giving up the
struggle to think about what I had learned.

Genia spent much of her free time with Nina, and
their conversation turned more and more on the subject
of the town; they were both determined to accompany
me on my first trip when the track was passable. I tried
to tell Nina that the town had changed, that it was a
ghost town, a dour trading post on the edge of the old
world, but she would not listen. They both insisted that

I, a man, could have no idea of what they were looking for, and that therefore I was not a reliable judge, but it was a subject that I did not like to think about. I felt sure that they would hate the town; and I felt somehow betrayed by their excitement and curiosity about it. It seemed to me also that they incited Rebecca to believe that she too could make a visit to the town, when obviously such an idea was impossible.

The situation troubled me because I could not see how it could be resolved. It added to my other concerns: my inability to shake off my intense longing for Christina, my worry about Frieda's health, and about the consequences for us all if the weather did not break soon.

But there were always occasions, events, encounters in every day which helped to restore my faith and my strength.

My bathroom was just off the studio and one day I wandered naked into the studio itself, forgetting that it was in a sense a communal room. At that moment Genia entered the studio and I remembered instantly the incident at the cabin when she had asked to see me naked; so I did not attempt to cover myself but stood quite still, the dog on hind legs. She stopped, stared at me, smiled, and then after a few moments burst into laughter. I went back into the bathroom and returned with a towel wrapped around myself, whereupon she flew at me, still laughing, and pushed me back onto the bed and sat astride me and pressed down hard on my shoulders.

"I suppose it is funny," I said.

"Thomas, Thomas, it was your expression, the expression on your face that made me laugh. Surely you did not think that it was the first time that I had seen you naked? I must tell you that within one week of coming to this house I had crept down to your room in the middle of the night and while you slept, pulled back the sheets to feast my eyes. I admit then that I was shocked, but I have grown used to the idea."

"Why then," I asked, "did you demand to see me naked?"

"Because, Thomas, I did not know whether you loved me or not. You seemed at times uncertain; perhaps you tolerated me as a child, but did not see me as a woman. You did not really look at me, or notice me. So I was forced to discover the truth for myself. And now you are afraid that I will run away to the town..."

She leant forward and kissed me on the lips, to silence me I think, to stop my protest.

"Yet you want me to be free, and I must be free. Is it not true?"

"True," I said.

She rolled off me, pulling me with her and we lay side by side for some time like lovers, staring at each other and smiling uncertainly; her sexuality was so strong that it could only be experienced as an intense love; a longing for her happiness, her well-being, a fervent wish that her life should be magnificent and glorious, free from all ugliness, anguish, and pain. Long after she had gone the blood still pulsed through my body, a body weakened yet cleansed by the energy required to transmute desire into a feeling close to ecstasy.

That night, as I considered whether to play chess with Frieda or to take yet another walk about the house,

Nina whispered in my ear that her celibacy was at an end, and would I not come to her room.

It was a wonderful love-making, and afterwards since the others had gone to bed and the house was ours, I suggested that we go down to the balcony room; there we took off our clothes again and put more logs on the fire. Here at last was the scene that I had dreamed of when alone in the cabin, the firelight reflected on her beautiful breasts; her body, strong and healthy, and made more desirable by our love-making. As I looked at her and loved her, I was reminded of the paintings of naked women in the books in the studio, famous nudes, and I felt that Nina would not age, but would remain as I saw her then; and therefore I could not possess her in time, that I could not possess her at all; that I would have to allow her to escape me, perhaps to return unexpectedly to surprise me one day, perhaps never to be seen again.

We talked long into the night. She spoke of Genia, of her great energy, and of her hopes and longings; of Rebecca, who had apparently performed a brief but wild dance on discovering that the hair on her thighs was falling out in great clumps; of Frieda, that I should face the fact that she was dying; of Bella, how she was ever present in the house these days and how she was obsessed so often with thoughts of Christina.

And she spoke too of Elena, of the changes that she had noticed. She thought that Elena and I "looked well together," almost as if we were sister and brother, albeit hesitant siblings who had only recently renewed each others' acquaintance.

It must have been almost dawn when she suddenly interrupted something that she was saying; she gripped my arm and held her head in a manner that suggested that she had heard or seen or felt something that disturbed her, something unusual.

"Thomas," she shouted. "It is warmer. Surely it has become warmer?"

Immediately I pulled back the curtains and flung open the window. We ran naked onto the balcony. It was not snowing, it was not even that cold, and the wind had dropped to a gentle breeze. In the east there was the first color of what would soon become a brilliant sunrise.

I went out at once for my walk. There was no doubt that the temperature was well above freezing; the surface of the snow was soft, and there were places where the bare earth was visible in the tracks that I had made on previous walks. The blocks of ice were melting. The snow was falling from the branches of the cherry trees, forming large hollows in the snow beneath. The entire scrub-land glistened and sparkled in the early morning sunlight.

By the time that the others had gathered in the balcony room for breakfast, there were already patches of ground that were free of snow, and small streams wound their way towards the river. The speed of the thaw was amazing to see, and the air of excitement in the house marvellous to feel; even Frieda came to the room for her coffee, and carried her cup to the window to watch.

If the thaw continued I saw no reason why I could not drive to the town on the following day to replenish our supplies. Immediately Nina announced that she

would come with me. Frieda suggested that if I was sure
that the road would be passable, then why did we not
break our fast that evening and consume in a fine feast
all the food that we had been forced to keep in reserve
in case the freeze continued. This was agreed, and the
various tasks of preparation were allotted.

When I went out again the sunshine was reflected
brightly by the snow that remained. I checked the truck,
that there was enough fuel to reach the town. I walked a
mile or so along the track to see if it had suffered any
great damage; but though it was extremely boggy it
seemed in fair condition and would be passable on the
following day.

It was wonderful to be able to walk about easily outside without having to struggle constantly through the
deep snow and without having to keep on the move
because of the extreme cold. Having returned to the
house I sat on the bumper of the old truck and thought
about the drive that I would make. It would be a practical challenge and I looked forward to it with pleasure; I
had had enough of driving only to the cabin and back
and I longed for the sensation of making a journey and
of achieving something. I felt excited and I felt well; it
seemed to me that the sun was waking up my body and
my mind, and my spirit seemed on the point of soaring
into the crisp, clean air.

I saw Rebecca sitting on a chair against the trunk of
a cherry tree and I went towards her. It was then that I
noticed Genia and Nina out in the scrub-land. They
were carrying baskets and leaning forward close to
each other, obviously gathering something from the
ground. According to Rebecca they were searching for

a particular type of small flower, for mushrooms, and for any kind of edible green leaf. I said that I thought there might be mushrooms but very little else, but I was proved wrong because they brought back a basket full of greenery, the first fresh vegetable that we had had for a long time. They found also in abundance minute flowers of many colors, all in tight bud.

As I watched them I saw Genia waving in the direction of the house, and looking up I saw Frieda and Elena standing at the window.

Rebecca and I walked very slowly around to the other side of the house, and though I kept enquiring if she was warm enough, or if she was tired, she assured me repeatedly that she felt perfectly well.

"I walk slowly," she said, "merely because I have been bedridden for so long. I am no longer ill, Thomas. Tomorrow I will go with you to the town."

I protested that it would be impossible to take her; the road was in a very bad state, there was a risk of getting stuck, the seats in the truck were hard and uncomfortable; but she would not listen. Genia, she announced, would also be going, and she and Nina were well able to take care of her.

Supporting herself against one of the columns beneath the balcony, she spent some time watching Bella on the sand bar as she tried to extricate various objects from the thawing blocks of ice.

"What will you do now?" I asked her.

"I have lain in that room for so long, waiting, listening to the sounds that came from Bella's room and the sounds that came from Nina's room. I have had to be patient, but now the waiting is over. Do you not see,

Thomas, that everything has changed, nothing can be the same."

I nodded to her, but I did not understand. Certainly I knew that her life was transformed, and that I had changed, that much else in the house had changed. But I did not see a clear image of the future. I looked forward to the evening and I was excited about the drive to the town. But as to the future, I suppose that I imagined merely a better, truer, more exciting version of the life that we already lived; I might make journeys, perhaps frequent journeys, but I would always return to what was in effect my home.

That afternoon I slept, a wonderful deep sleep with only half the usual number of covers and blankets piled on the bed. Afterwards I stocked the balcony room with logs, and in the basement I cleaned and prepared the last few bottles of the good wine.

When I went into the balcony room in the evening it had been transformed; the small flowers that Genia and Nina had found were everywhere and had opened to reveal their bright colors. There were colored candles burning recklessly on the table, on the mantle, and on every other available surface. The table itself was laid with all the best cutlery, china, and glass.

Frieda wanted to sit near to the roaring fire and so Elena sat at the head of the table. I sat at the other end, with Nina and Bella on one side, and Frieda, Rebecca and Genia on the other. Though we were well spaced it was perhaps necessary since every available inch of the table was covered by the plates and bowls of the feast that had been prepared.

There were two kinds of soup, one the color of a dozen different pulses, the other a dark green, and they contained the last of all the vegetables. Nina had gathered together the remnants of many different flours and had baked a large and magnificent last loaf of bread. There was also a wonderful salad in an enormous bowl in the center of the table; the fresh, bright green leaves that they had found, and the subtle colors of the wild mushrooms, and the last three peppers, one green, one yellow, and one red.

We ate quietly and slowly, relishing every morsel, and no one could speak a word.

Finally there were apples; not a piece, but a whole perfect apple each.

When we had finished, Bella rose solemnly to her feet. She said that the spring had come because of the moon, that we should praise the moon, the beautiful moon.

We pulled our chairs back from the table and Nina put on some music; it was a strange dance music, semiformal, and played by some sort of country orchestra. She began to dance and shortly afterwards Genia joined her. At first they danced as a couple but soon broke away to dance their individual movements.

I watched them and I watched the others as I sipped the wine. Frieda seemed well content, and with her foot she tapped out the rhythm of the music. Soon Bella joined the dance, and even Rebecca with Nina's help began to move with amazing agility around the floor.

When I looked at Elena as she also watched the dance, I saw that her expression was one of amusement and curiosity perhaps, but also of detachment; and in some way it seemed to echo my own feeling. Was this indeed a feast, a celebration; and if so what was the element of finality and sadness that I perceived and felt even as we ate the good food, even as they danced?

I looked about the room, at the uncanny beauty of the flowers in the candlelight, at the roaring fire, at the crude, green-stained woodwork of the doors and windows; the grandeur and spacious dimensions of the room. At the women dancing and at the old woman, her arms gripping her chair, her feet tapping; and at the young woman, withdrawn, silent, as if anxious or afraid.

At the very moment at which this fear, if it was fear, might have communicated itself to me and over-whelmed me, at the instant that the wine might have turned to acid in my stomach, I was approached by Genia, followed by Nina, encouraged by Bella and Rebecca, and dragged to my feet and pulled into the dance. Within moments I was twirling and leaping and cavorting with them, being passed from one to the other, sensing the lightness of Genia in my arms, the strength and joy of Nina, the pleasure felt by Rebecca, and the tense sensuality of Bella.

When finally I slumped into a chair, sweating and exhausted, Elena brought me my glass of wine and stood behind my chair; with her fingers she seemed to play with the hair at the back of my neck. I realized that my hair had grown long and I resolved to get Nina to cut it when I returned from the town on the following day.

It was typical that though the weather had improved, we should on that night have a power failure; but the discovery was made in time so that a few candles could

be saved. We each took one and made our separate
ways to bed.

It was a calm night, there was hardly a wind at all.
As I lay awake I thought about the next day, about the
drive to the town, about buying vast quantities of provisions, and I realized that in some ways I had enjoyed
our siege, and that I was not overjoyed that it was over.
I confessed to myself too that the drive would not in
reality be a particularly purposeful act, but would
merely be a pleasant substitute for the mournful drifting
and uncertainty that had dominated so many of my
days recently. Lying there, unable to sleep, I sensed the
gradual disintegration of my world. I allowed doubt to
undermine my perception of the truth; the path of truth
was, as always, too difficult and too disruptive, too risky
and too painful.

Needing solace, I thought of the café in the town and
wondered if I would be able to get away from the other
women and go there and sit at the back, take out my
wallet and stare at the old photograph and let my mind
fill with melancholy. Yes, I would go there, of course,
and sit in my usual seat in the dark corner; and I would
see what happened, how events would unfold...

There was a gentle tapping at my door. I called out
to whomever it was to come in. Elena came into the studio, and stood close to my bed; she was wearing a black
silk dressing gown that reached to the floor, and her
hair was loose on her shoulders.

"Tomorrow, Thomas, I can help you search for
Christina."

I was completely taken aback by this offer, hardly
able to believe my ears; but I did not see now how it

would be possible to accept it. I told her that I must go to town as had been planned, but she replied quietly that there was no reason why Nina could not drive the truck.

"We must search for Christina tomorrow, Thomas. It must not be delayed. We must begin early."

"Of course, of course," I said. "This is wonderful news..."

She said no more, but turned and left the room; and from the bed I watched her bare feet moving beneath the black dressing gown. She stopped at the door and looked in my direction for a few moments before she disappeared, closing the door soundlessly behind her.

There was nothing else that could have been offered to me that would have given me such joy and excitement; I could not believe that Elena herself would help me in the search for Christina. I would not be alone, my strength would be doubled, and surely she must be found.

I wanted urgently to go and see Frieda, to talk to her about all this before tomorrow, but I felt sure that she would be asleep and I did not want to disturb her.

Eleven

The sunrise was even more spectacular than it had been on the previous day. Before the others were up I made myself coffee and then went on my usual walk. The snow had completely melted and the ground was much drier; I considered it quite possible that Nina could manage to drive the truck to the town. As I had expected, the river level had risen slightly, and I was pleased to see that it was washing away some of the rubbish that had accumulated on the sand bar and in other places near to the house.

On my return I made more coffee and took it to Frieda's room. She was already sitting up in bed and reading. She took off her glasses and motioned to me to sit on the bed beside her.

"You know that Elena is coming with me to help search for Christina?" I said.

She nodded. "Listen to me, Thomas. You must trust

Elena, and believe in her; try to see her as she is, a woman who would help you. You have in the past despised each other, and you are both stubborn; but you must now learn to become allies."

"We have become close to each other," I said. And I added as I left the room, "Will you be all right here alone for the day? Is there anything that you need?"

"I need nothing," she replied. "I have things to prepare, Thomas; rest assured that I shall be content."

There was great activity near to the truck at the back of the house. Rebecca bundled up in masses of clothes was being installed on the front seat, Genia had already climbed up behind the cab, and Nina was waiting for the rest of us to climb on the back before she raised the tailboard. Before setting off for the town she had agreed to take Elena and myself to the edge of the forest. She drove slowly towards the cabin, circled it, and stopped on the track facing the way she had come.

Having hugged Genia, I climbed down and began to remind Nina about the track into town; to watch out for large potholes, to keep an eye on the lower edge of the road in case there had been subsidence, and to go gently on the tarmac section because it might still be icy. She got down from the cab and embraced me.

"We will be fine, Thomas, fine. But you must look after yourself."

As she drove away with Rebecca smiling beside her, she gave long blasts on the horn. And as the truck disappeared the last thing we saw was Genia sitting precariously on the roof waving with both hands towards us.

I had assumed, I think, that Bella would go to the town with them, and I was surprised to find that she had got off the truck. Carrying her sack as usual, she was now wandering near the forest's edge. I turned to Elena, and she to me. It was the first direct acknowledgement of each other that day. She wore at least two skirts, the top one being a pale yellow color, and a padded jacket, and these clothes combined with the walking boots completely belied her slender form, making her seem almost stout and strong. Bella, wearing only a coat thrown over a long thin dress, seemed inappropriately dressed for a long day's searching in the forest; but perhaps she did not understand what we were there to do.

I said that I would collect the rope from the cabin, but Elena laid her hand on my wrist and said quietly that we had no need of it. I explained to her that my idea had been to follow the rope until it ran out, and then for one person to stay by the end while the other searched the surrounding area, thereby searching much more thoroughly than I had been able to do on my own. And now that there were three of us... But she stopped me, simply repeating that there was no need for the rope, and that I was to trust her.

I knew that as soon as we entered the forest the dangers would become clear to her, so I held my peace.

As we moved amongst the trees and boulders and ferns, Bella was always at a distance from us, sometimes ahead and sometimes behind us, sometimes wandering slowly as if in a dream, sometimes running; and often she stopped to pick up something, inspect it, and place it in her sack if it was to be kept.

Elena, in the lead, walked resolutely forward at as fast a pace as was possible in that terrain, and she did not seem to look to left or right; she proceeded as if she knew her way and was clear about her objective. After about ten minutes I called out and when she stopped I drew level with her. With a sweep of my hand I indicated the forest around us, and asked if she did not now see that every direction seemed identical except for the slightest change in the light in the direction of the cabin; did she not understand that if we went on like this for much longer we could so easily be lost? She allowed me to finish; and then in the same quiet tone of voice she said that she knew which way she was going, and that I should have no fear of being lost.

But I could not allay my anxiety. I knew how easy it was to lose one's way, and throughout all my years in the house I had learned to be wary of the forest, to understand that to penetrate beyond its edge could lead to catastrophe. Following Elena, I began to stumble and fall quite often and to bruise my ankles and knees simply because I was unable to concentrate my mind on negotiating the boulders and creepers and the mass of fallen branches.

I called out to her again and again she stopped; but when I came up to her I was trembling and had to ask her to sit down with me so that we could talk. She sat crossed-legged against a tree and I knelt down close to her. Bella also came and sat near to us.

When I tried to talk I realized how completely the fear had taken possession of me; I tried desperately to explain to her that I was not frightened of the forest itself, nor of injury, nor even death, but I was terrified of being lost; of being cast adrift forever in a world that had no meaning. But my words only increased my trembling, as if I did not expect to be understood, as if I made my predicament worse. I could only repeat that I was terrified, overwhelmed with fear, and that I could not go on. And I pleaded with her to return with me now to the cabin while there was still a chance of finding our way back.

For some minutes she was silent, waiting for me to calm myself.

"We cannot go back, Thomas," she said quietly.

As I heard these words I leapt to my feet, determined to retrace my steps even if I had to go on my own. But looking about me, at the identical trees, at the strange pyramids of boulders illuminated by the pale green light, I knew instantly that I was already lost. It was too late. I had not a clue which way we had come. I sank to my knees, and fell forwards with my head in my hands, silently cursing my stupidity.

"You must simply abandon your fear and have faith in me," she said.

This sentence she repeated several times as I lay there; and the word that echoed in my mind was "abandon." Relinquish, yield, flow, what did it matter now. I ceased to shake, and slowly regained control of myself.

Bella moved close to me and opening her sack, spread the contents on the ground; amongst the pieces of string and shell and driftwood were all the small objects that I had given her that belonged to Christina. For a few moments I stared at these things, and then carefully I picked up and held each one in the palm of my hand before replacing it in the sack. I closed the drawstring and passed it back to Bella.

We walked then for two hours without stopping, and at no point did Elena hesitate in her onward march. It was at this time that I began to notice that the forest was changing, the trees being less tall, and the undergrowth becoming more varied and luxuriant. And a short while later the sun's rays began to slant down through the branches, dispelling the gloom and shining on the small white flowers that were underfoot and on the green and red and brown of the leaves of the trees.

We emerged suddenly from the wood at the edge of a small escarpment and found ourselves overlooking a most perfect valley. We lay down to rest and to look. There were small flowering trees dotted at random on a brilliant green sward; here spring was well advanced, and everywhere there was the flight and sound of many many birds. The air was clear and the breeze seemed warm. In the valley below a small river flowed over waterfalls and the banks were lined with elegant gray trees that were laden with red berries.

Immediately below us, and at no great distance, there was a pool formed in the river, and there was some disturbance to the surface of the water; as we watched, a figure began to rise, and the water that cascaded free of the body was bright and translucent in the sunlight. As she climbed from the pool she shook her head and her fair hair shed the water like ribbons of gold. She was beautiful and naked, so much more beautiful than I remembered, her body perfect and pure in every part. She reached forward to pluck up a leaf that floated on the water; and as she sat down by the pool, peacefully studying this leaf, I realized that her sight had been restored.

Looking at Elena lying beside me, I knew beyond any doubt that she too perceived this beauty, and shared my feeling; that we looked together upon the most perfect form of beauty. When instinctively I began to get up to go to Christina, I was not surprised that Elena caught hold of my hand to restrain me.

"She cannot be touched," she said to me; and though every fiber of my being longed to approach her, to speak to her, to see her eyes upon me, nevertheless I understood in that moment that it was not possible.

We watched for a long time and when at last we rose to leave, we saw Bella running down through the trees towards Christina; though she still carried her sack, she had thrown off her clothes, and she moved swiftly over the grass in long, magnificent leaps and bounds.

As Elena and I turned back into the forest I felt exhausted and emotionally drained, and I was apprehensive that she could lead us back to the cabin; but immediately she set out with confidence on an unwavering course. She did not look back, but occasionally she shouted out to me to keep up, to keep close to her.

The trek took longer than on the outward journey and as I walked I wondered at the image of Christina that I carried in my mind; though I had not spoken to her, I had seen that she was alive, that she was happy. Her image was at ease within the beautiful scenery of the valley, and therefore I could leave her, all longing and desire, anxiety and fear fading from my mind.

When at last we emerged from the forest, I saw in the distance beyond the cabin a strange reflection of

which I could at first make no sense. But slowly it
dawned on me that what I was seeing was a vast lake
that reached within two hundred yards of the cabin
itself. The river had flooded its banks and engulfed the
house. I could not see clearly so I scrambled onto the
roof of the cabin and helped Elena to climb up after me.
The ground floor of the house was obviously totally
inundated, but I felt sure that the water had not reached
to Frieda's room.

It was a strange sight, and it took me some time to
take it in; one of the boats had been lifted from the cove
and now floated aimlessly between the top most
branches of the cherry trees. There were small waves
lapping at the stone walls of the house.

But as I watched the whole house seemed suddenly
to vibrate as I imagined it might have done in an earth-
quake. Only one end of the balcony was visible from
our position, but I could see clearly that one of the supporting columns was beginning to buckle and subside. It
seemed as if the balcony itself might tear clear of the
house, but it hung there for some time as if floating on
the water. Then the entire house skewed sideways and
twisted itself in slow motion; and silently, slowly, the
building collapsed and disappeared completely beneath
the water.

In my panic I called out Frieda's name, scanning the
surface of the water, half expecting to see her hanging
onto some piece of furniture and calling out to us. But
there was nothing. The surface of the water eventually
calmed and continued its headlong course, surging
about the trees, carrying its usual burden of detritus; it
was as if the house had never existed.

We stood balanced on the cabin roof for some time, slowly accepting the fact that Frieda must be drowned; that we had arrived just in time to witness her death, and to realize that her body had been swept away in the flood.

That evening as we waited in the cabin for the water level to drop, I tried desperately to recall the last words that she had spoken to me that morning; her words and the expression on her face, her glasses perched on her nose, her frail hand patting my arm as she spoke.

But the river level did not go down that evening and we were forced to spend a sad night in the cabin. I lit a fire, and we ate a small meal with the food that I had left there. We slept together in the one bed, lying close to each other, quietly talking until we fell asleep. I dreamed that I saw the mouth of the river just as the flood waters reached the delta; I saw Maria's boat lifted from a sandbank where it had been stranded and I saw it carried far out to sea.

We awoke to a gray, dismal day; the water had receded and the river now flowed almost exactly in its normal channel. We made our way to the house and though I had expected the area to be deep in mud, it was not so; indeed it was difficult to believe that the scrub-land had been under water at all.

The house itself had collapsed completely and was an utter ruin; but it was strange that though the material of the house, the actual stones and mortar and timber and glass were strewn about and heaped up in great jagged piles, there was no sign of the objects and stuff of our occupation; no signs of furniture or curtains, or

cooking equipment or any of the mass of other things.
In places the rubble had been spread about the smaller
trees and it was as if these saplings had grown up
through the wreckage; it was as if the house had been
ruined for many years.

And nor could we discover the body of Frieda.

We wandered there for some time in silence, turning
over stones, lifting pieces of timber, unable to believe
what had happened. At the cove great boulders had
been rolled up onto the beach; and in the cherry
orchard we saw that the upper branches carried a burden of twigs and straw and rubbish left there by the
flood. The boat had failed to escape the net of trees and
had settled at an angle against one of the trunks.

When I walked a short distance along the track in
the direction of the town and saw the remnants of
smashed boulders that littered the carriageway I realized that Nina and the others would be unable to get
back to the house. It was only then that I considered the
possibility that there had also been floods further downstream at the town and that therefore there was reason
to fear for their safety. But I dismissed this thought,
being convinced that the flood had only occurred near
the house because of its unique situation, the sand bar
and the bend in the river. Nevertheless we would have
to join them in the town as quickly as possible, and I
went back to the cherry orchard to inspect the boat to
see if it could be used.

It was a heavy boat and seemed to have survived its
battering. It would only be necessary to row clear of the
bank because if I used the tiller carefully, the flow
would easily carry us downstream to the town.

When we first tried to move the boat it was too heavy for us. We collected pieces of branch and any other timber that we could use as rollers. While Elena transferred these branches from back to front under the boat, I managed to heave it slowly around the side of the house and across the sand bar to the edge of the river. I explained to her that I would row as far as I could out into mid-stream and that she must use the tiller to steer the boat constantly clear of the bank.

By the time that I had recovered my strength sufficiently to attempt the rowing, we were enveloped in a damp mist that began to blow in dense clouds from the river. Together we pushed the boat into the water, and climbed aboard. At once I began to row as hard as I could towards the center of the river. When I considered that we were a sufficient distance from the bank I slackened my pace; and a little while later I stopped rowing altogether and shipped the oars.

I slid backwards off the seat and slumped exhausted in the bow of the boat. I could see very little, and hear only the lapping of the water against the sides of the boat and the muffled gurgling sound as it passed over the rudder. Occasionally I spoke to Elena, asking her to keep an even distance from the bank, and to tell me the moment that she sighted the town. She nodded in reply, though she stared into the mist with unseeing eyes.

As I watched her I wondered what she was thinking; about Frieda perhaps, or Christina, about the loss of the house; or perhaps about our future. Her face was wet from the mist, and her eyes seemed to shine. Her fine hands grasping the tiller seemed to have no strength, no substance; she is not dispirited, I thought, but preoccupied, as if anxious lest a cherished plan fail to come to fruition.

When some time later I sat upright and looked about me I could no longer see the outline of the bank of the river. Clearly Elena had steered us much too far into the center of the river. But gradually I became aware of what had happened; she had managed somehow to steer the boat across the river towards the other side. Whether she had done this intentionally, or by accident because she was in a dream, I could not tell, but I knew instinctively that we had crossed to the other side. Already I was sure that there was no possibility of going back.

She saw that I realized what she had done, and she watched me closely to see how I would react. I felt only a fleeting sickness in my stomach, a panic for a moment that I was not yet ready to abandon our world; yet at the same time I had a sense of great peace and calm.

"And Genia and Nina and Rebecca, what of them?" I asked her.

"Let them go, Thomas. They must go free, let them be free."

I sat back again in the bow of the boat; and though I felt that I would be unable to sustain the feeling, nevertheless for the time being I gave myself up to her mercy. The sensation was unique to me, the strange awareness that my trust in her was absolute, as if I understood that she could value my life as much as she did her own. And I knew that whatever happened to us, we could not deny this collusion; we could not be denied its power.

As I watched her I saw her face suddenly brighten, and lifting myself I looked from the bow of the boat.

Through the mist I could make out the yellow lights shining through the windows of houses; and then more clearly I saw quite close to us a harbor wall. But no sooner had I glimpsed it than it began to slip away from us into the mist and I realized to my horror that the river was sweeping us on past it and that it was too late to attempt to guide us in using oars and tiller.

Then we heard voices and the sound of the engine of a boat, people shouting to us, asking if we spoke English, speaking about us so that we heard distinctly what they said: "Are they from the other side?" and then, "Of course, look at their clothes." Then there were words directed at us, soothing words: "Don't be frightened. You're very lucky, we sighted you just in time."

In the boat there were two men and they came along side and fixed a tow-rope to the bow of our boat; they maneuvered away from us into the mist and after a few moments I saw the rope go taut and felt our heavy boat being drawn slowly through the water. The mist seemed then to intensify, and at times it was difficult even to see Elena sitting so close to me.

The towing took a long time, and it was not until I saw that we were passing very close to the outer wall of the harbor that I began to take stock of what had happened; that we had been rescued, if that is the right word, by these two men who seemed to be sailors; that they were taking me back to the harbor of a village of a country, of a world, on whose soil I had not stepped for many years; a place from which I had once fled in horror.

I was surprised at the depth of my curiosity about this land, and surprised too that I felt no fear.

As we turned at the end of the pier to enter the harbor itself, I was amazed to see that there were colored lights along the entire crescent of the bay; and these lights moved in the breeze, sending out sharp lines of bright color into the misty air.

It was while I was absorbed in watching these lights dancing before my eyes, that I heard Elena speak from the stern of the boat. I was vaguely aware that her hair had come loose from its plait and was being gently lifted in the wind. It was not easy to hear what she said because the engine noise was deflected back at us by the stonework of the wall.

"We cannot be seen together," she said. "You understand that, Thomas?"

At that moment they began to push and pull our boat in towards the harbor steps, and I could not think what she meant. On the pier were a great number of people, all excitedly looking down at us and talking loudly amongst themselves. First the bow of our boat swung against the steps, and then the stern, and then the bow again before it was finally brought under control and tied up; and in the confusion I could not see Elena. I got out and began to climb the stone steps that were old and worn and soft. As I neared the top I came level with a yellow dress and then saw the bright smiling face of a young woman. She seemed excited to see me, and placed a garland of flowers about my neck; she kissed me almost passionately on both sides of my face.

In the crush of people I could not find Elena and involuntarily I spoke her name aloud; and at once she replied, saying, "I am here." It was clearly her voice as if very close to me, even though I could not see her. I said, "We have arrived," but it was the young woman who had greeted me who replied: "Yes, yes," she said, "Welcome, welcome," and she gripped me by the arm so that we would not be separated in the jostling mass of people on the pier.

There was great interest in our boat for some reason, and they fixed a hoist to it and were lifting it from the water. When they set it down on the pier they crowded about it, full of admiration and curiosity. They chattered loudly and jovially. They ran their hands lovingly over the carving at the bow and the stern. And it was then that I noticed that the tiller had been tied firmly in the center of the boat by two brightly colored scarves.

The young woman, still holding tightly onto my arm, guided me away from the crowd and along the pier in the direction of the village. She walked briskly, swinging her hips, still apparently overjoyed at my arrival.

"We have a hotel room for you tonight, and tomorrow..."

I did not hear what she said. I looked up at the sturdy white houses built on the hill that surrounded the harbor and I too felt something of her excitement.